MURDER MOST MADDENING

A CAROLYN NEVILLE MYSTERY BOOK 3

JOHN DUCKWORTH

Murder Most Maddening
John Duckworth

Print Edition

CKN Christian Publishing
An Imprint of Wolfpack Publishing
5130 S. Fort Apache Rd. 215-380
Las Vegas, NV 89148

eBook ISBN 978-1-64734-701-7
Paperback ISBN 978-1-63977-094-6

MURDER MOST MADDENING

To my wife, Liz, who believed it was worth trying.

PROLOGUE

THE COLORS WERE CHANGING FASTER NOW, NOT THE FAMOUS fall colors, but the colors in his head, blending. Opalescent greens, sulfur yellow, a pure, prismatic blue. The moonlight showed him the girl emerging from the woods, weaving her way on the trail through a stand of aspen, the leaves fluttering like sparrows.

Her very proper blouse and skirt certainly fit her profession. But her hair was just askew enough to tattle on her. Probably coming back from a meeting with one of her boyfriends, he thought. Nobody would suspect it, not of this girl. But it wasn't safe for her to be out this time of night, not when there were people who might not be responsible for their actions.

People like him.

At first the acid had been a very spiritual experience, opening him up to the universe like a columbine in the sun, but by the third trip everything had gone wrong. His head seemed to turn inside out, his eyeballs twisting backward, confronting his own brain. There was too much in it. *She* was too much. Something dangerous about her. Couldn't put his finger on it.

Maybe he could use his hands instead.

The trail crunched louder under her shoes. She couldn't see him behind this swollen pine. The smell of pitch was in his nose, the tacky syrup sticking his cheek to the bark. His head kept expanding. He was going to turn to vapor. Had to act while his body was still solid.

Like a stray thought she swished past. He watched his arms shoot out like jack-in-the-boxes, triggered by someone else with a secret name.

He did what had to be done.

He fixed things. She made a noise, of course, but not much louder than the trees.

After that, he ran into the darkness. His legs had always been strong.

After that, he could never remember how far he ran, or where.

CHAPTER 1

HUNTER THICKE HAD BEEN ASKING FOR IT. IN FACT, HE'D demanded it.

That's why I was still in Manhattan on a Friday night in July, trapped with nearly a hundred coworkers in the banquet room of a once-great hotel, the Handover Arms. I was chewing the kind of chicken that tasted like rubber tire patches in a briny gravy, studying half a dozen infrequently dusted chandeliers that dangled over my head like Damoclean swords.

Stephen Ames, my junior-aged senior editor, leaned toward me from his chair. "Don't be nervous," he whispered.

"Don't be silly."

He shook his head. He'd worked for me long enough to know how much I hated public speaking. Unfortunately, this was a command performance, for a cause I opposed with every ounce of my strength, which was considerable for a woman who felt opening stuck pickle jars qualified as cardiovascular exercise.

"It'll be over before you know it," he added. He picked up his goblet of ice water with the calm of one who, unlike me, wouldn't be getting up in 15 minutes to face a multitude. It was no fun addressing an audience that would rather be dipped in honey and staked to an anthill than attend this event.

He was, in his flip, millennial way, doing his best to be supportive. It was the least he could do, considering I'd kept him off the list of hapless employees dragooned into publicly praising a man who'd made all our lives miserable.

I wondered which bootlicker in the room had arranged this. Not that I could do a thing about it.

The podium stood empty, waiting. I'd be the initial after-dinner speaker, followed by a parade of unlucky colleagues. Why I was scheduled first was anyone's guess. Maybe the planning committee wanted to start with the weakest act and save the best for last.

Stephen glanced toward Hunter's table, just in front of the dais. "*He* seems to be having a good time. Which is more than I can say for Candace."

The latter was Hunter's wife. We weren't used to seeing her. She sat next to him, his opposite in most ways. He sprawled in his chair, one arm angled over the back, a paradigm of posture. His frat-boy grin was disarming; her smile was warm as a dermatologist's blast of liquid nitrogen. From what I'd heard, all they had in common was their Gen-X credentials, *Vanity Fair* wardrobes, and production of a toddler they'd fobbed off on a nanny the minute she'd left the hospital nursery.

And their ambition. Candace, a corporate lawyer, was said to harbor political aspirations. Hunter, meanwhile, wanted to be CEO of anything that moved.

"Wonder how she feels about this," Stephen said, keeping his voice low. "It's not every day your hubby celebrates five whole years in the same job. What staying power."

I shook my head. Ridiculous, celebrating such a molehill

of a milestone. What was it compared to my 15-plus years at Pendleton House Publishing? How about the much longer sentences other employees had served? Hunter was a relative greenhorn, a tyro, a novice. Many colorful nouns could be applied to him, but I couldn't do that out loud. Supervisors weren't supposed to use such language about the vice-president of content development, especially when surrounded by potential backstabbers.

By the time dessert came, I was checking my watch every 30 seconds. The bubbling in my stomach didn't keep me from eating my soggy square of cherry cobbler, though. I told myself the sugar would keep me from fainting when I ascended the platform.

At precisely 7:14 p.m. the podium was seized by a woman I didn't know. Her face looked vaguely Italian. Her practiced smile was that of someone offering free guacamole samples at the supermarket, pretending they were her life's passion but already thinking about her next job.

"Now that we've had some incredible food and conversation," she said, "let's get to the business at hand."

Hunter put down his fork and paid rapt attention. Candace folded her hands next to her cobbler plate.

The emcee smoothed a sheet of paper on the lectern. "Since 1899, Pendleton House Publishing has had a rich history of forward-looking men and women who sought to bring great literature to the world." She glanced up, as if for assurance that she'd pronounced all the words correctly. "These men and women were pioneers. Our guest of honor tonight is the latest to join that august body." She said *august* as if it were the month. I shook my head, mourning for civilization.

Hunter looked down modestly at his plate, his slicked-back black hair catching the light of the chandeliers. I consulted my watch, counting the minutes left until my humiliation.

"Five years ago," the woman continued, "Hunter Thicke came to Pendleton House after six years in research and marketing at Chronicle Merkel, our parent company. Immediately he reinvented the Editorial Division by renaming it the Content Development Division." She paused, giving us a chance to let this achievement soak in. "As if that weren't enough, he outsourced e-books to India."

I looked at Stephen. We both knew how well *that* was going. Let's just say it wasn't.

The eulogy shambled on, until the woman at the podium clutched a dramatic hand to her chest. "A groundswell of employees asked for the chance to thank Hunter for his leadership. Tonight is the result." She wanted to thank the planning committee for its craven servility, which she pronounced as "hard work."

A second later I heard my name. My heart beat faster.

"Since Hunter arrived, he and Editorial Director Carolyn Neville have worked side by side."

I frowned. Too close by several feet. She also didn't mention how many times I'd drafted my resignation and torn it up.

"And now," she said, "Here's Carolyn to tell us about the *real* Hunter Thicke."

I swallowed. There was a spatter of polite applause. Rising, I caught a glimpse of Stephen, his smiling face framed by an Ed Sheeran thicket of caramel-colored hair.

That was when it came to me.

What if I were honest about the real Hunter Thicke? What if I left my notes in my purse and spoke the truth about just how uncomprehending and devious our leader was?

Not point-blank, of course. I'd make it sound like a compliment. A few in the audience would understand and snicker. When I was done, all would rise for a standing ovation—a few because I'd done the impossible, and most because they thought it was mandatory.

I dismissed the thought immediately, of course. There was a reason I was still here after all these years. It was a simple matter of my retirement account, interest rates, and a whole lot of subtraction.

I returned to reality in time to hear the applause die. As I made my way to the front, the only sounds were a few tinkling glasses and stifled coughs.

Placing my papers on the lectern, I took a deep breath and began.

I won't describe the speech that followed. Let's just say that for the next six minutes I touted Hunter's many nonexistent talents, lying through my teeth.

The big finish was a quote from Francis Bacon, which I've blocked from my mind along with the rest of the presentation. Later I burned my notes in a coffee can on the balcony of my condo, destroying the evidence of this wretched episode forever.

There was no ovation when I finished. Only a repeated impact of the palms, barely enough to allow me to sit down.

"Nice," Stephen whispered.

I shook my head. "It was a disgrace."

"You did what you had to."

"I didn't have to lie. It's the eighth commandment. Or the ninth, depending on your denomination."

"You couldn't tell the truth. Nobody could."

A couple of employees at nearby tables gave us the sort of frowns one gives in a movie theater to those who think popcorn is a percussion instrument played with the teeth. I settled back in my chair.

I looked over at the Thickes. Hunter was smiling at me.

Then he winked, which only made it worse.

* * *

There followed the inevitable lineup of speakers, most of them sounding like captives forced to read statements about how humanely they were being treated.

The exception was Norton Sturbridge, the senior vice-president Hunter reported to, a patrician gentleman whose perfect mane of silver hair matched his Ivy League accent. He drizzled faint praise on his protégé, calling him "energetic" and "quite skilled with a nine iron." He also took the opportunity to remind everyone that budgets were tight this quarter, and to cut costs by reusing paper clips and tipping less on business lunches.

Finally the moment for which few had been waiting arrived. Hunter himself mounted the platform, grinning and shaking his head amid the less than thunderous applause as if to say he couldn't believe the little people loved him so.

When he waved, the clapping quieted. He thanked the planning committee, his boss, and his wife, who acknowledged the mention by tilting her head to one side and blinking.

Unlike most of the other speakers, he took no notes from his pocket. His tendency to orate off the cuff was well known to those whose ears he'd commandeered in one meeting after another.

"Friends," he began, apparently addressing a constituency unable to attend, "what a wild ride it's been. When I came to this company five years ago, I had no idea what a privilege it would be to serve with you. Some had warned me the folks at Pendleton House were resistant to change. But I learned quickly that, as the well-known author and submarine captain Mark Twain said, reports of your depth had been greatly exaggerated."

He paused for a response, but no one seemed to know

whether he'd mangled the quote on purpose, or that he'd mangled it at all. Or that Mark Twain had been a riverboat pilot, or that he was known as Samuel Clemens at the time. A few people coughed again, that being the universal sign for uncertainty.

"It reminds me of a story," he said. Several sighs were heard in the audience, at least one of them from Stephen.

Our leader lowered his brows, maybe to indicate earnestness, or to help him remember what he'd read in that 20-volume library of anecdotes we all imagined he kept on a shelf somewhere. "It's the story of a man who brought change to a nation that needed it desperately. He cut unemployment by eighty percent in six short years. Workers got vacations for the first time, even free trips to the beach. He advanced animal rights, set hunting seasons to limit killing, and put endangered species on a protected list."

Pausing, he squeezed one eye shut as a memory aid, then pressed on. "This man banned smoking in restaurants and on public transit. He started one of the biggest welfare programs in history. He set up the world's first freeways and paved the way for exploring space. He urged the production of a car everyone could afford, even suggesting its shape, and it became one of the most popular vehicles in the world. Who was that man?"

Silence.

"Adolf Hitler!" He threw his arms wide.

The silence grew longer.

"No, the guy wasn't perfect. But who is?" He smiled. "When it comes to change, let's follow in his footsteps. Will you join me?"

Glancing around, I saw others glancing around.

He seized the flanks of the podium. "Ladies and gentlemen, the first five years were just the beginning. Let's march fearlessly into the future together. Today, Manhattan . . . tomorrow, the world!"

The applause was slow to get started, and quick to stop. I looked over at his wife. She was rubbing her forehead, eyes closed.

Stephen half-covered his mouth with his hand. "God help us," he murmured.

When it was over, the two of us I sat there while the tables were cleared. I was too tired to get up, and both of us knew traffic would be a mess.

"A night to remember," he said.

"I hope not."

"Five years," Stephen said. "Seems longer."

I crumpled what was left of my napkin. "The lady who empties wastebaskets in our department has been there for about forty. And look at Marvin."

"As in Marvin Ainsley Pitts?"

"We're coming up on the fiftieth anniversary for *Darkness at Dawn*. In about eighteen months, I think. A great book."

"Well, you *would* say that. He's your friend."

"You've read it. You know what it's like."

"Sure. It was a bestseller, but it's not selling anymore, is it?"

I sighed. "No. If it loses any more steam, we'll have to let it go out of print. We can keep it as an e-book if Marvin doesn't want the rights back, but it deserves better. *He* deserves better."

He picked at a spot of cherry cobbler drying on the tablecloth. "Don't we all." He looked at his watch. "Well, it's been fun. See you in five years."

"We should do a revised edition of that book," I said, watching him get up.

"Revised how? The murder happened almost fifty years ago."

"But it was never really solved. Marvin had his theory, but couldn't prove it. Maybe he could come up with a new angle. Long-lost DNA evidence or something."

He shook his head. "You're talking about a huge amount of work. Marvin's retired. And not recently, either. Probably doesn't want to take on something like that."

"That would be up to him. Besides, you know what Hunter's always saying about the vast treasure trove."

Stephen rolled his eyes. "He may *think* we're sitting on all this fabulous content we own the rights to, if we'd just repurpose it. He may *think* we can turn magazines into apps and make books into musicals. But we usually *don't* own the rights. And when we do, we've already recycled most of it. Five years, and he still doesn't know half of what we've published."

"All the more reason to do something with Marvin's book. We still own it."

"I'm not the one you have to convince. But good luck getting it past Hunter, much less Marvin. And good luck getting back to Connecticut before midnight." He turned and headed for the exit.

Twisting in my chair, I watched him go.

It was a long shot, the idea of updating Marvin's book.

But I couldn't let his real accomplishment be eclipsed by Hunter's fake one.

Especially when I'd helped fake it.

* * *

Hunter had always called them one-on-ones, these Thursday morning meetings. I suspected it was one of those sports analogies he loved so much, the one-on-one having something to do with basketball, a diversion I followed as closely as I did the ancient Mayan game of Pok-a-Tok.

This week, though, we weren't meeting in his office. We were sitting in the Pendleton House cafeteria, The Golden Quill, at a round table someone had recently wiped with a dripping washcloth.

Even more unusual was the fact that this was Hunter's idea. Clearly something was up.

He stirred two packets of sugar into his coffee, then set the cup down next to his iPad. I stirred mine for no particular reason, then placed it next to my notepad and pen.

"I bet you're wondering why I suggested meeting here," he said.

I folded my hands on the table. "You're letting me go and wanted to do it in a public place in case I got violent."

He chuckled. "Not this time. Wanted to thank you. For what you said at the banquet the other night."

I cocked an eyebrow. Maybe this wouldn't be the best time to recant my remarks.

"What you said was right on. Set the tone for the whole evening. I had no idea you felt that way about my approach to management."

Neither did I, of course.

He gazed across the mostly unoccupied seating area. "Sometimes I wonder, Carolyn, whether all my effort is worth it. The meetings. The travel. Telling my admin to send flowers when somebody's Aunt Tillie dies. It never ends."

I nodded, filled with something less than admiration.

"But when you and the others laid your hearts bare, I gained the strength to keep going."

I frowned. If only I could turn back time.

"Candace said afterward she'd never seen such an outpouring of gratitude from a group of employees. It made me want to pay it forward. Hence the coffee."

I looked down at the cup. "Very generous," I said.

He nodded, then picked up his iPad and started poking it. "Now, about these returns on the Mortimer book—"

I held up my pen. "Before we get to that, I wanted to bring up a related point. About anniversaries."

"Yours? How many years are we talking about? I can't be expected to remember—"

"Not mine. We're coming up on the fiftieth for *Darkness at Dawn*."

He thought for a moment. "*Darkness* . . . Oh, right. The one by your friend. The black guy."

"Marvin. I was thinking we could do a revised and updated edition."

"Oh? Let's take a look." He started prodding his iPad again, then winced at what he saw. "With sales like these, I can't believe it's still in print. After we sell the stock in the warehouse, we should send it to that big remainder bin in the sky."

"But it's a classic."

"So's the Volkswagen Beetle. Which was the car Adolf Hitler designed, by the way. You don't see anybody revising and updating *that*, do you?"

"Actually, a few years ago they—"

"Carolyn, nobody cares about stuff that happened fifty years ago. There's no reason to think revising the book would make it do any better than it's doing now."

"But what if the murder were finally solved?"

He put the iPad down. "What murder?"

I rubbed my temples with my fingertips. "Have you ever read the book?"

He shrugged. "Maybe not the whole thing."

"It's about a killing in a little town in Colorado. Somebody strangled a young lady, a schoolteacher everybody loved. Made national news at the time. They never caught whoever who did it."

"And now somebody's going to? How?"

"DNA evidence, maybe. Exonerates people all the time. Even on death row."

He shook his head. "I get that Marvin's a friend of yours, but—"

"What about the treasure trove?"

He hesitated. I could tell he wanted to choose his words carefully, so as not to contradict his previous infallible declarations.

"As you've so wisely pointed out," I said, "there's a vast reservoir of intellectual property beneath our feet. This book is one example. Think of the possibilities."

He picked up his coffee and took a sip. "Movie?"

"Exactly."

He paused, tapping a finger on the table. "We'd have to bring it up at the next sales conference. Get their reaction."

"Naturally."

"Even if they say yes, we couldn't spend much time or money on it. You heard Norton Sturbridge at the banquet. We can't even throw away paper clips."

"Marvin would do all the work. We make a few phone calls, draw up a contract, offer him a small advance for research. Give him six months. If he doesn't come through, the project is dead. And the book goes out of print."

He nodded slowly. "I like the sound of that."

I leaned back in my chair and folded my arms. "What could go wrong?"

He picked up his iPad again. "Don't let me find out," he said.

* * *

As soon as I got back to my desk, I dialed Marvin's number.

"That you, Cranberry?" came the familiar voice. We

hadn't talked in a while, but I could still hear the twinkle in his eye, so to speak.

"How's St. Petersburg?"

"Hurricane season. Florida's a treacherous place."

"But you're a treacherous man. That's why I have a proposal for you."

"Girl, if it's in the center of God's will for you, I'm all for it."

"Can't guarantee that. I'm not as spiritual as you are."

"Now, don't let those Manhattan materialists get you down. I don't know how you can go to work every day knowing the folks around you think you're a snake handler or something."

"They don't. Or at least most of them don't seem to hold it against me." I loved Marvin, but I didn't want to have this conversation again right now. "It seems you have an anniversary coming up," I said.

He paused. "I do? My lovely bride and I have been together forty-three years, but I thought it was in February."

"I'm not talking about your wedding anniversary."

"Thank the Lord. Forgetting is a hanging offense around here."

"Do you remember when *Darkness at Dawn* came out?"

"Sure. I was at the *Tribune.* Cubbies were third in the league. Ernie Banks was playing infield. You were probably in kindergarten."

"Almost fifty years ago, Marvin. That deserves some attention."

"From what I've seen on my last three or four royalty statements, not everybody would agree."

"That's why we'd like to do a revised edition. Update it. Get it selling again."

He went silent for a few moments. "Cranberry, are you messing with me?"

"I wouldn't dare."

"Let me ask Tracy."

There was a jostling sound, and his wife's muffled voice. Then more jostling.

"She says you're pulling my leg. Or just humoring an old man."

"No to both," I said. "Strictly business. And a little art."

"Truth is I've always wanted to fix that book. It left everything up in the air. Even if nobody wants to read it, I'd like to write it."

"All you have to do is figure out who killed Iris MacIlhenny."

"Well, yeah. Girl deserves justice. By all accounts she was a real sweetheart."

"You thought it might be the mine owner."

"Franklin Gant. This time maybe I can prove it."

"With DNA?"

"Don't know. But forensics has come a long way in fifty years. It would take some travel, though. Fees for lab testing. Expenses."

"We can give you a small advance."

"How small?"

"Let's say five thousand."

He grunted. "Let's say seventy-five hundred."

"Sold."

"How long would I have?"

"Six months. I know you hate instant books, but it's not a new manuscript. Just a revision."

"How much new content we talking about?"

I thought fast. "About . . . twenty percent."

"Six months, huh? Guess I can live that long."

"If you're worried you won't, I can put a rush on the contract."

"Good idea. Like Tracy said, I'm an old man."

"One more reason to do the book. While there's still time."

"I'll do my best, girl."

"You always do." I paused. "Keep an eye on your mailbox for that contract."

"Right."

I pushed the END button.

Guess I can live that long.

I shook my head. What a joker.

Everybody knew Marvin Ainsley Pitts would live forever.

CHAPTER 2

WEEKS PASSED. THE PROJECT'S WRINKLES WERE IRONED OUT well before Labor Day, just in time for the Coney Island fireworks and the parade of pugnacious union members on Fifth Avenue that always looked more like a lynch mob than a festive occasion.

Marvin flew to Colorado, touching base by phone every seven days. I conveyed his progress to Hunter in our one-on-ones, which no longer involved The Golden Quill, coffee, or the words *thank you.*

* * *

It was also the time when my friend Mikki Flaherty decided we should get together again but wouldn't tell me why. As usual we met at Roundelay's, the doughnut place near my condo and her townhouse in Connecticut.

"So what's this about?" I asked, sticking a straw in a carton of milk.

"It's not what you think," she said. She brushed her bangs, which were the size of robin's wings, out of her eyes. They were strawberry blonde this time. I hadn't seen her in bangs since last year, when they were jet black. Rearranging and dyeing her hair is kind of a hobby, along with scarf dancing on the worship team at church.

"What do I think it is?" I asked.

"You think I'm trying to set you up on another awful blind date."

"You're not?"

"Of course not. This'll be a ten."

I shook my head. "You said that last time."

"He's a guy from church, a lawyer. And he's tall."

I picked up my doughnut, a chocolate-iced chocolate with chocolate chips. "If he's so great, why don't *you* go out with him?"

"I'm seeing somebody else."

I almost dropped my doughnut. "Really? Who?"

"His cousin. He's more my speed. An Uber driver."

"What's so great about this lawyer?"

"He's a professional, like you. Looks a little like a young Dick Van Dyke. Funny like him, too. Very sincere. I'm a good judge of people, despite the trail of crappy relationships I've left in my wake."

"Did he *ask* you to do this?"

"No, his cousin did."

I took a big bite of doughnut and chased it with milk. The sugar rush almost made me pass out.

It also affected my judgment. "All right. I'll do it. I'm not desperate, but maybe he can afford a decent restaurant."

"You won't be sorry. I'll give him your number."

I told her about Marvin's project. She shuddered when I described the MacIlhenny case.

"Too creepy," she said. "But good luck with the book."

"We'll need it. Hunter's not being very supportive."

She dunked her maple bar in her coffee. "Never is, is he? Kind of like my boss, but with hair."

We talked for another half hour or so about the usual gripes, then picked at the crumbs on our napkins. "His name is Jim," Mikki said.

"Who?"

"The guy you're going out with."

I'd already forgotten. The sugar was wearing off, and I felt a lot less optimistic.

"Nice name," I said, getting up. If this one didn't go anywhere, I'd never say yes to her again.

Until next time.

* * *

Marvin's reports continued like clockwork. He was still a little woozy from the altitude, he said, but things were moving along nicely.

Stephen and I plowed ahead with our regular fall season of acquisitions and releases, locked in the traditional death match with our fellow employees. On a sunny Tuesday in September, we found ourselves in a titling meeting, Conference Room 3C. It had been called by a new brand manager in Marketing, a nervous-looking woman whose arms seemed to exist solely to display her extensive collection of bracelets. This was an emergency, she said, handing out strategy statements for a newly contracted book with the working title *New Bryn Gibson Project*.

The two-page document was typical, chocked with buzzwords like Psychographics and Cover Hierarchy. The book had something to do with the author's journey of spiritual discovery and a potbellied pig called Farley.

"This one fell through the cracks," she said, her bracelets clacking as she stacked the leftover sheets of paper. "Need a cover by Friday for the catalog. Designer's got to have a title by end of business today. Put on your thinking caps."

"I like the working title," I said.

Her forehead furrowed. "Are you serious?"

An old hand from Publicity, a rumpled fellow whose first or last name was Dean, glanced up from reading. "She's not used to you yet, Carolyn. Give her a break."

"I mean it," I said, putting down the paper. "We're about to throw ourselves into a marathon of brainstorming. Somebody will stand at the white board, covering it with columns of iffy suggestions. Somebody else will keep checking Amazon to see which titles are taken, eliminating at least thirty-five percent. Then come endless rounds of crossing out and circling and voting and re-voting, rearranging words, commenting about this title not promising enough and that one promising too much, and recycling the also-rans into subtitles.

"In the end we'll compromise on one nobody really likes, no better than the working title. You'll e-mail it to Hunter, who'll veto it, and another meeting will be called at 4:59 p.m. to come up with a replacement."

Stephen stifled a grin. The new Marketing lady looked around as if trying to gauge majority opinion by expressions or body language. But most around the table were frowning studiously at the documents in their hands.

"Okay, then," she said brightly, picking up an erasable marker. "Let's begin."

There was a pause. "How about *Farley and Me*?" someone suggested.

"Too much like *Marley and Me*," The Marketing lady said.

I looked up at the ceiling tiles.

That's when I heard the *1812 Overture*, my ringtone, jangle from the pocket of my tweedy brown blazer. I cut the sound, then checked the number.

"It's Marvin," I whispered to Stephen. "We should take this, don't you think?"

"Yeah, and for as long as possible."

We slipped into the hallway, then into the empty Conference Room 3D. I shifted the phone to speaker.

"I'm back in Florida, Cranberry." He sounded a little tense.

"You okay?"

"Sure. Just checking in."

"Are you done in Colorado?"

"Done? No. But I've made headway. Mostly in the last few days."

There was a pause.

"So tell us, already," Stephen said. "What did you find out?"

"Well . . . some very interesting things."

Another pause.

"Okay," I said. "You're building suspense. Using a fiction technique in a nonfiction context. That's why you won that Edgar award."

"Not trying to be suspenseful. Just can't be too specific yet."

"Why not?"

"Can't be too specific about that, either. Let's just say this may be the revised edition to end all others."

"Marvin, you're driving me crazy."

"Yeah, I'm sorry." He paused. "I *can* tell you this: People aren't always as they seem."

"Profound," Stephen muttered.

"Are you sure you're all right?" I asked.

"Yeah, girl. I may be old, but I haven't lost my touch. I should be able to tell you more next week."

"Yes, but—"

"Gotta go. Don't worry. It's all good."

There was silence on the line.

I looked at Stephen. He looked at me.

"Marvin was always a bit dramatic," I said.

Stephen checked his watch. "Can we skip the rest of the meeting?"

I shook my head. "Love to, but we have to limit the damage. That's one of our books they're talking about."

We walked across the hall, opened the door, and pretended everything would be just fine.

* * *

That night, back in my condo, I sat at the kitchen table after dinner. The place still smelled of ginger and garlic, thanks to the leftover beef stir-fry I'd microwaved. I stared at the bookshelves lining the living room walls. Almost as many volumes as the nearest branch of the Hensford Public Library, and much more wisely chosen.

I fired up my laptop. To my left lay the strategy statement for the *New Bryn Gibson Project,* which the titling committee had cleverly redubbed *Farley's Way: The Wise Woman's Path to Hog Heaven.* To the right, face down, was my copy of *Darkness at Dawn,* the first edition hardcover, autographed by Marvin and inscribed "To my favorite Cranberry. God bless." Farther to the right was half a glass of Louis Jadot Chablis 2015, which went perfectly with the dish of candy corn in front of it.

I had a strategy statement of my own to write. Sales conference loomed in just three days, and Hunter expected me to push the salespeople toward a favorable forecast for Marvin's revision. Without their blessing, the product would never clear the launchpad.

The first section on the form said PROJECT HISTORY. Simple enough. I'd use the same case I'd made to Hunter.

New York Times bestseller, critically acclaimed, nearly a million copies sold. Its central mystery still unsolved, but up for grabs in the digital age. I wanted to make this part longer, but the sales force wasn't famous for its patience.

Then came SUMMARY. I thumbed through the book again. Little mountain town in Colorado, mostly mining. Iris MacIlhenny, 26, taught all subjects to third and fourth graders at tiny Motherlode Elementary. There was a photo. Attractive, slender, porcelain complexion, dark blonde hair, blue eyes. Kids and townspeople loved her.

Brutally strangled.

I shook my head, then thumbed some more. The town was more or less built around a gold mine owned by the Gant family. Marvin's theory: Franklin Gant, 40, a married mainstay of the community, was infatuated with Iris. She rejected him; he attacked her in a rage. There was a photo of Gant, too. Short, stocky, meticulously groomed, imperious, no smile.

But not everyone bought Marvin's explanation. Here was a shot of Sheriff P.J. Boyle, late thirties, squinty, hair like closely mowed straw, slightly irregular good looks. Described by Marvin as a blunt pragmatist with no patience for the "hippies, vagrants, and drug addicts" who drifted in and out of the mountains.

One such drifter was an aspiring flower child who called himself Skye, a young man with no last name, apparently a college dropout. He blew into Motherlode one summer, two months before Iris was killed, and disappeared a few days after her death. No photos were available. Sheriff Boyle told anyone who'd listen that he suspected Skye. But nobody knew who he was or where he'd gone.

When I got to the section that said AUTHOR BIO, I knew Marvin's by heart. Grew up in Kansas City. B.A. in journalism from Lincoln University, Jefferson City, Missouri.

Started out as a crime reporter at the *Chicago Tribune*; graduated to big-league true-crime books with this breakout bestseller. Another eight books since then, most of them with Pendleton.

The rest of the strategy statement was about hype: Author Platform, Facebook, Media Contacts. I doubted Marvin had any of those. So I said he'd be happy to blog, even though I was sure he'd rather drink molten lead.

When I got to Possible Endorsers, I paused and bit my lip. Most of the blurbs on the book were from people who were dead or wouldn't be recognized by anyone under 55. Did Marvin have any famous friends who were still alive? I couldn't make them up. I needed real names.

After finding my phone, I called his number. It went directly to voice mail.

I hung up without leaving a message. For a second I felt a twinge, a chill. I told myself he was fine. He was Marvin. It was all good.

I threw myself into working and reworking the whole thing, trying to make the project sound like a cross between *In Cold Blood* and Laura Ingalls Wilder.

The whole thing took about 90 minutes. When I was done, I rewarded myself with the last of the candy corn.

Finally I looked over at my phone, wishing it would ring.

It wouldn't.

* * *

It did, though, the next night.

"Hi," said a male voice. At first I couldn't place it, then realized that was because I'd never heard it before.

"This is Jim Farris. I think we have a mutual friend. Mikki Flaherty."

Aha. Sounded like a lawyer. Definitely tall. Very sincere. As for the sense of humor, I couldn't tell yet.

"I love blind dates, don't you?" he asked.

"Sure. They're like dancing in the dark on the tollway."

He chuckled. "Are you up to this?"

"What did you have in mind?"

"I was thinking of dinner at Red Lobster and the new Benedict Cumberbatch movie."

I cocked an eyebrow. "Did Mikki tell you those are two of my favorite things?"

"Maybe."

"That's cheating, but okay."

"I understand you don't get home from work 'til 6:30. Pick you up tomorrow at 7:00?"

"I'll be here."

He was five minutes early, which counted in his favor. As far as I was concerned, punctuality had been dropped from the Ten Commandments only because those stone tablets weren't big enough.

He was a few inches taller than I, but not the Yao Ming that Mikki had led me to envision. I had to remember what a hummingbird she was.

His smile was warm, his frame a little thin but broad-shouldered. Thick, brown hair was brushed back from his forehead but not glued there like Hunter's. His outfit was almost all denim, and his hands were in his pockets.

So far, so good.

I hadn't been to Red Lobster for at least a year, but they still had Lobster and Langostino Pizza. Langostino's a shrimp that looks sort of like a hairless caterpillar, which isn't nearly as revolting as it sounds. They also had those crusty, buttery, garlicky golden rolls that come in a little basket. I had both, which meant I'd smell like an Italian restaurant dumpster for the next 24 hours. Jim and I wouldn't get close enough tonight for it to make a difference. We'd more or less met at church, after all.

He ordered Citrus Rum Grilled Mahi Mahi and a house salad. "I'm sure the alcohol cooks away," he said, the way some of the faithful feel compelled to do.

"So you're a lawyer," I said, already looking for another napkin thanks to those toasty, oily rolls.

"Mostly tax cases. You wouldn't believe what the government tries to do to some perfectly innocent people. It's kind of a crusade with me."

A crusader? Well, I couldn't fault him for that. I was pretty much trying to save the civilized world, one aggravation at a time.

"And you're an editor. *That* must be interesting."

"It has its moments. Or so I'm told. I've only been doing this about twenty years, so I figure the fascinating part must be just around the bend."

"I suppose it's tough being in a high-pressure place like that. Having to keep your emotions in."

My brows lowered. Red flag number one went up.

I cleared my throat. "If you mean all women are ready to burst into tears at a moment's notice, I'll have to disagree."

He shook his head. "Not at all. Just that they're usually more sensitive, right? Not dumb blocks of wood like us guys."

There went flag number two. Pretending to put down men to justify putting down women. And we hadn't even gotten our food yet.

"I mean, look at the science. It's not politically correct to say so, but—"

Suddenly he stopped and looked down at the roll on his plate. "Arguing's a plus in my line of work, but not when I'm dining with a very charming lady. Can we start over?"

"Well, maybe."

"This is probably why my cousin wanted to set me up. He knew I hadn't gone out in at least six months."

"Neither have I."

He looked relieved. "Then it's not as pathetic as I thought?"

I gave a little smile. "It is, but at least we have it in common."

We both settled back in our seats. For the time being, I put the flags away.

The rest of the evening went pretty darn well, if you ask me. We talked about everything from Mikki's Uber-driving boyfriend to the question of who knew more about the legal profession, Scott Turow or John Grisham. We even touched on a little God talk but steered clear of the whole women's-role-in-the-church thing.

When it was over, things happened the way I'd thought they would. We didn't get close enough for our two garlic breaths to become one.

But there was always next time.

CHAPTER 3

THEY CALLED IT AN "OFFSITE," WHICH WAS A MEETING unnecessarily moved to a place at least a hundred times more expensive than a Pendleton conference room. Preferably one owned by a friend of a board member and paid for by recycling paper clips.

In this case it was a retreat center called The Barns, 45 minutes north of Manhattan. It had been an actual farm at one time, judging from the shape of the bright red buildings, the rooster weathervanes, and the game of horseshoes in the middle of the circular driveway.

I parked my RAV4 in front of a white picket fence. Stephen and I had avoided being trapped with Hunter by convincing him not to carpool with us. Our relief was disappearing quickly, though.

"Sales conference," Stephen said. "Hate it."

"A necessary evil," I said.

"A dog and pony show. You stand in front of about forty Sales and Marketing people, knowing they're going to tune you out after the first thirty seconds."

"Try tossing handfuls of candy bars into the audience. Gets them on your side."

"I've never seen *you* do that."

"I try to maintain a little dignity. Besides, it doesn't work. They get excited for a minute or two, but not about the book."

He looked in the mirror of his visor and combed his hair with his fingers. "So how are you going to get them cranked up?"

"Charm. I brought the house down at the banquet, remember?"

"Seriously."

I looked out the window at a pond on our left. For a moment I wondered whether the ducks floating on it were real or plastic.

"Seriously, I don't know. The strategy statement is okay, but it's not enough."

He looked at his watch. "We'll find out pretty soon. Right after the backslapping, bad jokes, introductions, and complaints."

"I see you've been here before," I said, and climbed out of the car.

* * *

Things went fine at first. Stephen's predictions about the agenda were more or less accurate. First came the shrinking band of road warriors who still called on brick-and-mortar stores in their territories, hugging each other and saying they were getting too old for this crap. Then the gripes of Marketing millennials who didn't like the descriptions of our books on Amazon. Then a few remarks from Hunter, who must have been inspired by the setting to tell a story about George Orwell's *Animal Farm*. He thought it was a children's book we could turn into a Saturday morning cartoon.

"And now," he said, extending a hand in my direction, "our editorial director, Carolyn Neville, has something to share with you."

The applause was energetic, the whistling likewise. The rowdiness faded as Stephen handed out copies of the strategy statement.

"What, no PowerPoint?" someone cried.

"This proposal practically sells itself," I said.

"Nothing sells itself. That's why *we're* here."

There were two laughs, a snort, and several knowing nods.

"I'll give you time to read the Summary section," I said.

"Hope you've got all day," a woman mumbled.

I heard two *Tsks*, a *Hmm*, a faint moan, and saw some shaking heads. "Sad story," someone said.

"Any questions?" I asked.

Silence filled the room like nerve gas.

Stephen, looking anxious, raised a hand. "I hear the author's already uncovered some very interesting surprises about this case."

"Like what?" somebody asked.

"We don't know yet," I said.

Stephen tried again. "I hear he says this could be the revised update to end all revised updates."

"What does that mean?" somebody called.

"We should know by next week," I said.

Hunter didn't look happy. "Let's move on to the rest of the statement."

More silence, more reading, more moving lips.

"I don't see anything under Possible Endorsers," said the Marketing woman.

I studied my nails. "To be determined."

Then came the chorus of harpies.

"Carolyn, this all happened half a century ago. You won't get anybody my age or under."

"Or over, either. I don't care what happened in the sixties, except maybe the Beatles and Pop Rocks."

"Pop Rocks were in the seventies. Invented in the sixties, but—"

"Sad commentary, but anything less than a mass shooting these days is small potatoes."

The Bracelet Lady stood up. "I suggest we give this some thought through the weekend. Then e-mail me with your vote." She gave her address. There were some nods and *uh-huhs*.

"Sorry, ma'am," somebody said. "We still love you."

The clapping sounded like a consolation prize.

"Thank you," I said, and sat down next to Stephen. I tried to look hopeful but couldn't pull it off.

The Bracelet Lady moved on, hooking up her laptop and flashing the rush-job cover of *Farley's Way* onto the projection screen. It pictured a pig's foot, or maybe a pig's arm, pointing the way into a white-hot burst of light. The rushed designer must have been ready to slash his own throat with an X-Acto knife.

"Too much pink," somebody said. "Men won't buy it."

"They won't buy it anyway. It's for women."

When the verdict came, it was the usual: Go back to the designer and try again.

For the next three hours the group staggered through discussions, breakout sessions, and empty promises. When the afternoon was gone, the Bracelet Lady dismissed us for dinner. I felt a tap on my shoulder.

It was Hunter. His hands were in his pockets, a Mona Lisa expression on his face. "We'll talk Monday," he said flatly.

I swallowed. "Yes. Let's."

He walked away with the others. Rumor had it a real farm-style dinner was about to be served, whatever that was. Something from KFC, probably.

"It's all over," I mumbled to Stephen.

For once he didn't contradict me.

* * *

The room emptied. I stood and stretched and sighed.

"I don't want to call Marvin. He'll be so disappointed to know his work is going down the drain."

"So don't," Stephen said.

"Have to. Don't want him to waste more time on it. Maybe I can give it a positive spin."

I took out my phone and dialed, hoping but not hoping he'd answer.

It rang once, twice, three times. Then he picked up.

Only it wasn't Marvin. It was his wife.

"Is this Carolyn?" she asked, her voice shaking.

"Tracy, what's wrong?"

Stephen's eyes grew wide. I put the phone on speaker.

"I'm . . . with Marvin. We're at the hospital."

"What's going on?"

"This afternoon, about two o'clock. I came home from shopping, found him in his office." The tremble in her voice got worse. "Face down on the floor, like he'd tripped on a rug or something. Blood on the back of his head."

She paused. I heard something beep steadily in the background.

"Didn't know if he was alive or dead. Paramedics said he was alive, praise God. But we've been here since then, intensive care."

I closed my eyes. "Do the doctors know what happened?"

"Only that there was a hit to his head. From behind. Hard, obviously."

"I'm so sorry. Have they said anything about what to expect?"

"They say he's in a coma. Can't get him to wake up. Even if they could, they don't know whether he can . . . come back. Really come back, you know? Whether he'd be himself."

I shook my head. "Is there anybody there with you? Anybody who can help?"

"I called our pastor. He's coming later. Called the prayer chain at church. Left messages for our kids, but they're so far away. Son in Houston, daughter in San Francisco."

The beeping resumed in the silence.

"Is there . . . anything we can do?" I asked.

"Pray."

"I sure will."

"The Lord is a very present help in trouble, Carolyn."

"I know."

"Though to tell you the truth, I've never been so scared in my life."

"Neither have I," I said, then wondered if I shouldn't have said it out loud.

"I'd better go. Nurse has to do something."

"We'll call tomorrow," I said.

"Yes, fine." The line went silent.

So did I.

CHAPTER 4

I SAT BACK DOWN. THE ROOM SEEMED SLIGHTLY CROOKED. When I placed the phone back in the pocket of my blazer, the tweedy part seemed rougher than usual against my fingertips.

"Maybe we should go outside," Stephen said. "Get some fresh air."

I stood up, my legs a little rubbery. I spotted the stack of strategy statements on the chair next to Stephen's. They may as well have been bus schedules now.

The sun was low in the sky, with a breeze that carried the crunchy, salty smell of fried chicken. My stomach growled, which seemed selfish under the circumstances.

"There's a bench by the pond," Stephen said gently.

When we got there, the slats were warm against my thighs. I stared at the water. "The ducks are real," I said.

"Did you think they weren't?"

"Couldn't tell."

We watched as a mallard with an emerald head dipped under the water and bobbed back up. *The duck ducked.* Was that where the word had come from? Maybe it was funny, but at the moment nothing was amusing.

"I wonder whether this has something to do with the book," I said.

He leaned forward. "Not necessarily. Could have been a burglary."

"You heard how he sounded a few days ago. Like he was worried."

"Yeah, I remember."

I looked down at my shoes. "Maybe he discovered something he wasn't supposed to know."

"But to hit an old man so hard you put him in a coma . . . that's not normal."

"Neither was strangling a grade school teacher."

"You think the same person did both things? Fifty years apart?"

I shrugged. "Don't know."

One of the ducks, a brown female, made a *raaaak* sound, flapped her wings, and seemed to be picking a fight with another that matched her. The noise seemed especially irritating.

"So what do you want to do?" Stephen asked.

"I guess all I can do is wait until tomorrow and try to get an update from Tracy."

"Makes sense." He paused. "Are you going to be okay?"

"Of course. Eventually."

He looked a little sheepish. "I'm sorry, but I'm really hungry. Hope you don't mind if I go to dinner."

"Go right ahead. I'm not ready to rub elbows with that group. Wouldn't aid the digestion."

He stood up and walked away.

I sank back against the bench and stared at the wildlife, which seemed to be calming down.

Marvin wouldn't like it here. Always itching to do the next thing. Not into pastoral settings.

He hadn't been raised in one, after all. He'd grown up in Kansas City, son of a joke-telling barber and a telephone operator who'd spent her spare time publishing a biweekly newspaper to help hold the black community together.

From the first time I'd met him, Marvin had seemed exotic. Being from Idaho, I hadn't known a single African-American until college.

Now I tried to picture him on the bench, tall and skinny, his long legs and tennis shoes stuck out on the sidewalk. He'd be making some comment about the waterfowl, maybe about how God had given them great instincts or how they were smarter than some people he knew.

I stretched my legs the way he would have, looking at the brown flats on my feet. He wasn't into dress shoes. Probably wore them to church to please Tracy.

I sent up a wordless prayer with my eyes open, not wanting to get too specific because I knew I'd start crying. But they welled up anyway, my throat clenched. Fishing a tissue from my purse, I felt the tears spill over and hoped everybody else was enjoying that fried chicken and not watching me.

I'd never seen Marvin cry. He didn't talk a lot about himself. Said plenty about Dr. King and Alex Haley.

It had taken a few years for him to tell me the rest, the parts that never made his bio. His two older brothers were dead, one shot in a drug deal and one stabbed by a gang member for no reason anyone could find. Marvin had gotten into trouble a few times himself, but nothing worse than a misdemeanor. Thanks to a teacher who saw his promise as a writer, he'd managed to stay out of the juvenile justice system. The United Negro College Fund had taken it from there.

I looked at the sky. The sun was even lower now, and I could still smell that fried chicken. I wondered what Tracy was eating at the hospital, if anything.

I got to my feet. *Sorry,* I thought. I had to keep going. We all did.

Even when you might lose the closest thing you had to a grandpa.

* * *

Saturday morning, back in the condo, I called Tracy. I waited until 9:00 in case she was sleeping. When she answered, her sandpaper *Hello* told me she'd been awake for a long time.

"Still in the ICU," she said. "Doctor Evans just came by with a bunch of medical students."

"What does he say?"

"Condition's unchanged. He could wake up today. Or never."

"Have the police talked with you again?"

"Not since yesterday."

"How are *you* doing?"

She sighed. "Holding up, I guess. Pastor came by last night. They may send two or three deacons this afternoon. Anoint Marvin's head with oil."

She paused, and I heard the steady beeping again. "I keep thinking of all the times I've nagged Marvin about one thing or another. I'm sure you've heard me do it. Wish I could take it back."

"I'm sure you had your reasons."

More silence, more beeping.

"Have you heard from your kids?"

She yawned. "Uh-huh. They'll come soon as they can. It'll be a few days. Can't afford those last-minute flights."

But I could.

She yawned again. The beeping was more prolonged.

"Sorry," she said. "I can hardly keep my eyes open."

"I'll let you go, Tracy. Sleep if you can."

"What? Oh, yeah."

The line went dead. Maybe she'd dropped the phone or pressed the wrong button.

She needed somebody there, someone to give her a break.

I looked at the clock over my stove. If I started now, I might be able to get a flight.

It would mean being out of the office Monday, when I was supposed to meet with Hunter. I decided to leave him a message. All I could get was his voice mail.

I tried to summarize what was going on. Surely even he could understand how important this was.

And if not, I didn't give a rip.

* * *

St. Petersburg General Hospital, like everything else I'd seen in Florida, was surrounded by palm trees and old people in sunglasses. Getting out of my taxi, overnight bag in hand, I paused long enough to miss the car's air conditioning.

The building in front of me was gray and glass and wide as a stadium. Walking between the squat pillars at the entrance, I took a last breath of muggy air and plunged into the cool of the lobby.

There were more old people inside, some visiting, some being wheeled out in chairs with little pennants on them. Not all the visitors were geriatric, of course. A family waited for someone, each member holding a blue balloon on a ribbon. But this was Sunday morning, not a prime time for callers.

After getting directions, I made my way past a garden of tropical turquoise, green, and purple chairs and took the elevator to the ICU. When the door closed, I sagged against the thrumming wall. Having left home at 3:00 a.m. and flown out of LaGuardia, I was still in the same time zone but felt jet-lagged.

A woman in blue scrubs sat at the nurse's station, writing on a clipboard.

"Looking for Marvin A. Pitts," I said.

She looked at her computer screen, then shook her head. "Patient's been moved to the general ward. Second floor."

"The general ward. That's good, right?"

"I don't know, ma'am. Generally speaking, yes."

The second floor looked much like the previous one, shiny tile and off-white walls. A man at the nurse's station pointed me toward Room 206.

The door was open. I hesitated, but only for a few seconds.

There he was, unmoving, his head padded with bandages, some kind of tube taped to the corner of his mouth. Three bags hung from his IV pole, all apparently connected to him. I saw the monitor I'd only heard on the phone, beeping like clockwork.

In an adjustable purple chair on the other side of the bed lay Tracy, her eyes closed. I hadn't seen her in a decade, but 10 years couldn't account for the sunken cheeks and the smudges under her eyes.

I set my overnight bag on the floor. When the zipper clicked against the tile, it was enough to send her eyelids up.

"Oh, my Lord," she said. She pulled a tissue from the box on the nightstand and dabbed at her lips, then managed a weak smile. "Carolyn, what are you doing here?"

"I heard you were having too much fun."

"Yes. That must be my problem."

Slowly she rose from the chair, grimacing. "I get so stiff on this thing." After tugging here and there on her navy-blue dress, she walked toward me, arms outstretched. When we hugged she smelled of rosewater, like my Aunt Gwyneth, and the musk that comes with having to skip a couple of showers.

"Thank you," she said. "You're the last person I expected to see this morning."

"Who was the first?"

"Mr. Nobody."

She returned to her chair. I took the smaller one on the near side. "I notice you're not in intensive care anymore," I said.

She nodded. "They say he's stabilized, doesn't need the ventilator to breathe for him. But they still can't get him to wake up."

I looked at the profile of Marvin's face. There was no movement at all, not even a rising and falling of the bedsheet. I'd have to take the monitor's word for it that he was alive.

"I feel strange not being in church on a Sunday morning," Tracy said. "Haven't missed once in at least a year."

"I'm sure the Lord understands."

She reached down to get her purse off the floor. "Care for a mint?" she asked.

I shook my head. "Have you had breakfast yet?"

"No, but it's almost time for lunch. I'll go down to the cafeteria when I get a chance."

"Well, you've got a chance now. I'll stay with Marvin."

"That's sweet of you. I wish he were awake so you could have a conversation."

"Take as long as you like. Take a walk, too, if you can stand the heat."

She got to her feet. "Oh, I'm used to that."

She paused in the doorway. "You know about the call button for the nurse, right?"

I nodded. "Don't worry."

When she was gone, I leaned back in the chair. Closing my eyes, I wondered why I'd been in such a hurry to get here. Marvin didn't even know I was in the room.

Or did he? I'd seen so many TV shows and movies where relatives and friends sat by a comatose loved one's bed, delivering a monologue in case he or she could hear.

I was considering doing the same when the *1812 Overture* pestered from my pocket. Checking the phone's screen, I saw Hunter's name and number.

Not now, not here. But I was the one who'd made a sudden departure. I picked up.

"Hunter," I said wearily. "Did you get my message?"

"You bet. Did you get mine?" He sounded impatient.

"You left *me* a message?"

"Last Friday, in person. After you crashed and burned at sales conference. We were supposed to meet today and pick our way through the ashes, remember?"

"As I said in *my* message—"

"No need to repeat it. Tough break for Marvin. I see why you want to be in Florida. But who's paying for this trip?"

"Who's *paying*?" I warned myself to keep my voice down, seeing that this was a hospital zone.

"We agreed not to spend much time or money on this project."

"We're not. I'm using vacation time. I'll pay the expenses myself. This isn't part of the project."

"Glad to hear it. How long before you're back in the office?"

"Two or three days." I found myself squeezing the phone a little harder than necessary.

"I want to see you in my office first thing Wednesday morning. About the project, but especially about sales conference. I can't have that kind of fiasco on my watch. Reflects badly on all of us."

By *us* he meant himself, of course.

Hearing the monitor beep in the background, I wondered why it was so lethargic. It wasn't keeping up with *my* heart rate or blood pressure, that was certain.

"Still there?" Hunter asked.

"Unfortunately, yes."

"Then give my best to Marvin's wife. Terrible thing."

"Terrible. Right." My grip on the phone grew tighter.

"Later." He hung up.

I looked at the phone, wanting to do something expressive with it. In the old days you could slam a receiver into its cradle with a sharp plastic *clack*. Now you could only stuff it in your pocket a little more forcefully than usual.

Which I did.

Bending forward in the chair, I looked at Marvin. I was poised to tell him everything Hunter had said, with searing commentary guaranteed to set off some sensor and bring the nurses running.

But what good would it do?

On the other hand, I had to say something. My face was hot and my pulse was stomping.

"Marvin, I'm sorry I got you into this." There went the tears again. I wiped them away with my hand, determined to keep going. "We need you to come back. The world needs you in it. God doesn't need you yet."

No reaction, of course. His face was almost gray, the color of cold coffee.

"We'll figure out who did this to you. And why he did it. Or she."

I wanted to promise. But I had no idea how to make good on it.

I shut my eyes and listened to the beeping.

CHAPTER 5

THE FOLLOWING AFTERNOON TRACY AND I MET OUTSIDE HER condo, one of at least a hundred beige units stacked eight stories high and surrounded by a battalion of palm trees.

Bending down, she collected a few editions of the *Tampa Bay Times* from the welcome mat, then unlocked the door.

"Have to get this fixed," she said. "Whoever broke in bent the lock or the door or something. Doesn't fit quite right, but the deadbolt still works."

When she pushed the door open, I could see the ocean view filtering through some kind of steel grates over the windows.

"Oh, I left the hurricane shutters closed. Still that time of year, but don't worry. Nobody's predicting anything."

Inside the air was hot and stale, but everything was tidy.

"Too quiet," she said. "Marvin likes to keep the radio going. I've heard more Nat King Cole and Barry White than I care to remember." She put her purse on the kitchen table. "Now, see? There I go again. He doesn't need me to criticize his music. He needs me to take care of him."

"The doctor said it was perfectly safe to leave for a while. You don't have to feel guilty."

She sighed. "I just want to take a shower. Do something normal, like vacuum the floor."

"Be my guest."

"You said you'd like to see his office."

I nodded. "You can just show me where it is."

"All right, but I have to warn you. There wasn't time to clean up the blood. The police didn't want me to anyway. Don't know how I'm going to get rid of it."

She led me down the hall to a converted bedroom. She hesitated for a moment, then opened the door.

There was a dark brown stain in the light brown carpet, right of center. It was smaller than I expected, about the size of a throw pillow.

"I'll go take that shower," she whispered, and left.

Except for the stain the room seemed clean enough, though not as orderly as the rooms under Tracy's jurisdiction. A desk with a computer monitor and Marvin's Edgar Award. Four black file cabinets, brick-and-board bookshelves. High school graduation photos of his kids. A Tampa Bay Rays calendar.

A framed copy of the *Darkness at Dawn* cover was on the wall, too, along with covers of three of his other books. So was a photo of a younger Marvin shaking hands with Alex Haley, both of them grinning, with Haley's autograph in the lower right corner.

There was one other photo next to it. I hadn't seen it in years. Marvin and I were standing just outside my Pendleton House office. I was holding up a plaque commemorating a million copies of *Darkness at Dawn* in print. He was making devil horns with his fingers behind my head.

Maybe I had a copy of the photo in a file somewhere, but

I'd never done anything with it. He thought putting his on the wall was important.

I cleared my throat, then decided to get down to business.

There was no point in looking for things like fibers and hair and footprints. The police knew what they were doing, and even if they didn't, I knew even less. I had to concentrate on information, any files or notes Marvin might have made on the revised edition.

I started with the computer, an aging Mac. When I booted up, it wanted a password. No doubt Tracy could tell me what it was, but she was in the shower.

I tried *Tracy*. Then *Lovely Bride. Darkness. Dawn.*

I rolled the old mouse on the pad, thinking.

Cranberry, I typed.

WELCOME, the screen said.

I sighed.

Using Searchlight, I hunted for files containing the phrase *Darkness at Dawn*. There were a few dozen, mostly correspondence about royalties or rights, standardized replies to fan letters, and contracts, all of them referring to the original book. No notes or content from the book itself, which made sense. There'd been no personal computers 50 years ago.

But there was nothing about the new edition, either.

Why? I wondered. *Unless someone deleted the files.*

I tried hard copies, rolling drawer after drawer from the cabinets. At least Marvin believed in the alphabet, which made things easier.

Under *Darkness at Dawn*, there was a solid foot of folders tabbed by chapter, plus places for Interviews, Photos, Permissions, Clippings, and Housekeeping. There was also a folder labeled New Edition.

It was empty.

I searched the desk. The only papers were letters from the

condo association, directions to a restaurant from Google Maps, and a notice about a class reunion.

Someone had erased all traces of the work in progress.

I sat in Marvin's desk chair again. Did the person who attacked him take the files? If so, why?

I got up and rolled out the cabinet drawer, then thumbed through the folders to Housekeeping. Among other things, there were three pages of names, phone numbers, and addresses.

Probably long outdated, too. I jotted some on my notepad anyway, starting with the sheriff's department and Franklin Gant, then Warner and Dottie MacIlhenny, Iris's parents.

I was still writing when I heard a noise behind me.

"Just me," Tracy said, looking slightly damp and even more slightly rejuvenated.

I told her what I'd found, or hadn't.

She shook her head. "I don't come in here much. I couldn't tell you where anything is." She paused. "Do you think this happened because of the book?"

"Pains me to say it, because I got him involved. But yes, if it weren't for me, he'd—"

"He'd be floundering around here, looking for something to do. When you called, he got more excited than I've seen him in the last ten years."

"Thanks for trying to make me feel better." I shut down the computer, then rose from her husband's chair. "Did the police find any fingerprints?"

"Not that I know of."

"Whoever got in here touched a lot of things. Must have worn gloves."

"The police don't seem to have found much of anything. Or if they have, they haven't told me."

I chewed at my lip. "I don't want to make you uncomfortable, but could you show me how Marvin was lying when you found him?"

She walked to the stain. "His head was about in the middle of that spot, turned a little to the right. His arms were kind of underneath, like he'd tried to keep himself from falling. It was a miracle he didn't break a hip."

I looked at the distance between the entrance and where he'd fallen. His attacker must have hidden behind the door and hit him when he came in. It was an ambush, not a case of being surprised during a burglary.

"Did he ever tell you how his research was going?"

"We talked on the phone every couple days when he was in Colorado. He had some trouble getting used to the altitude, but I could tell he loved being busy again. Didn't discuss the details. That's pretty much the way it's always been. I didn't bore him with accounting, and he did the same when it came to his work."

She took a last look at the spot. "High time I got that out," she said.

I picked up my purse. "And high time I got going."

We returned to the living room, where she gave me another hug. "God bless," she said. "Safe travels."

I stepped outside. She closed the door, wiggled the knob to make everything fit, and threw the deadbolt. The heat enveloped me like a second hug, but far less affectionately. I paused, pondering whether to turn right or left.

A sound came from inside the condo, faint at first, then unmistakable.

It was a radio, blaring Marvin's favorite kind of music, as loud as the speakers could make it.

* * *

I was waiting at the airport for my flight home when I got a call from Mikki Flaherty. Her boss must have been out. Otherwise, a personal call could have led to her summary dismissal, or at least a chewing out. But not getting called on the carpet. From what Mikki had told me, Icarus Imports had 100 percent cheap vinyl flooring.

"How did it go?" she asked eagerly.

"How did what go?"

"The date. You know, with the tall lawyer guy."

"Oh. It was actually okay."

"Are you gonna see him again?"

"Don't know. He hasn't called yet."

"So call him."

"I'm an old-fashioned girl. Besides, this problem with Marvin is keeping me occupied."

"The guy with the creepy book?"

I told her what had happened. My voice kept faltering, and I had to stop a couple of times.

"Oh, Carolyn," she kept saying.

"Mikki, it's my fault. I sent him out there."

"It is *not* your fault. It's the fault of whoever hit him."

"I just keep picturing him lying in that bed, helpless. Maybe never waking up."

She paused. "Did I tell you what it was like when my dad died?"

I searched my memory. "You said he had cancer, but I think that was it."

"Last time I saw him was in hospice then, at home. The nurse was great, but we all knew he was about to go. We came in one at a time to say goodbye. I was right after Aunt Becca. She came out sobbing. I went in. His eyelids kind of fluttered, but that was it. All I could do was kiss him on the top of his head. I still remember his hair smelled like ground pepper. Like some medicine was seeping out of his pores."

I swallowed, unable to talk. I turned away from the others waiting at the gate.

"I prayed for him," she continued. "As far as I know, he wasn't . . . you know . . . ready."

I sniffed. "Marvin's made his reservation. But I don't think he wants to go yet. Still has things to do here."

Neither of us said anything. I could hear the woman at the gate say it was time to start boarding.

Still holding the phone, I got up. "Time to go."

"It's gonna be okay," Mikki said.

"Yeah, I know."

But it sure didn't feel that way.

* * *

Two mornings later Stephen and I sat in Hunter's office. He'd volunteered to come along, irate at my account of Hunter's hospital call. Fine, I said, but he could speak only if the building came under terrorist attack. It was for his own protection.

Hunter sat behind his desk, facing away from us. Either he was fascinated with the construction site across the street or he'd read somewhere that such behavior would establish his dominance in this negotiation.

Slowly he turned around. Picking up a sterling silver pen, he proceeded to tap it on the arm of his executive chair.

"How's Marvin?" he asked.

"Out indefinitely. Maybe permanently."

"And his wife?"

"Brave. And grieving."

"Okay," he said, apparently glad to have gotten that unpleasantness out of the way. "Let's get down to brass knuckles. I need to know where this project is headed."

"How do you mean?"

"I mean I can't afford having you put time and effort into it. Look at the author. He can't possibly solve the crime now. The whole thing is over."

I folded my hands in my lap. "Maybe *we* could solve it."

"We who?"

"Stephen and I."

He shook his head. "Not on the company's dime."

"I've been thinking about that. I have about a month of accrued vacation time. I could spend it on this."

He shrugged. "Let's say I decide to approve that. I still can't spare Stephen. I need him to run your department while you're gone."

Stephen glanced at me, but kept his mouth closed. No terrorists had surfaced yet, unless you counted Hunter himself.

"Agreed," I said.

"Same schedule we've already settled on. You'll have to make up for lost time."

"Done."

He put the pretty pen down. "Now, let's move to what I really want to talk about. I think you know what it is."

"Sales conference."

"That's the one." He reached down and pulled out his top desk drawer, then took out something round, yellow-green, and fuzzy.

"Know what this is?"

"A tennis ball."

"Very good." Without warning he threw it at me. It hit me square in the forehead before I could get my hands up.

"*Ow,*" I said.

"Gotta think faster. Now throw it back."

I tossed it in his direction. He snagged it with one hand, not even looking.

"No offense, but you throw like a girl," he said, then

leaned back in his chair. "Carolyn, what's the First Law of Communication?"

I had no idea what he was talking about. There was no such law, not officially. I thought back to something I'd learned in Communications Theory class 40 years before and decided to run with it.

"Communication," I intoned, "is the transfer of information from one entity to another."

He shook his head. "Come on. You're supposed to be a communications gal." He lofted the ball a few inches and caught it in his palm. "The First Law is that you haven't communicated until the other person has received the message. I saw it on the Internet."

"Ah. *That* First Law."

He hurled the ball again. This time my hands shot up, but without effect. The ball bounced off the side of my face.

Scowling, Stephen opened his mouth as if to defend me.

I waved him off, then rubbed my cheek. Good thing I hadn't used much foundation that morning. "I was never good at playing catch. Do you know any other analogies?"

"No. This one is perfect." He paused. "Do you know how to tell the other guy's gotten the message?"

"He catches the ball?"

Leaning forward, he shook his head. "He doesn't fall asleep!"

"I . . . don't understand."

"Obviously. At sales conference you were putting those people to sleep. You and your strategy statement. What did you *expect* them to do?"

"Read it."

"Your first mistake. Nobody reads anymore."

"I keep forgetting."

"Give me the ball."

I walked it to his desk and placed it exactly in the center.

Picking it up, he proceeded to lob it in Stephen's direction. He caught it with both hands.

Hunter smiled. "I bet *he* knows what to do next."

And so he did. After rearing back, he hurled the ball straight at Hunter's head. Bullseye.

"*Ow*! Holy crap!" Hunter's hand went to his left eye. "What's the matter with you?"

"Just sending a message," Stephen said politely.

I was torn between scolding him for breaching our verbal contract and pumping my fist in victory. Compromising, I shifted slightly in my chair and kept quiet.

Hunter picked up his desk phone and pushed a button. "Janice, can you get me a bag of ice?" He paused, listening. "Just get it, okay?"

He hung up and covered his eye again. "Gonna need a freakin' patch," he mumbled.

"Sorry," he said. "Guess I throw like a guy."

Our leader took his hand away from his face. His eyelid was barely reddened. "My point, Carolyn, is that you need to become a more effective communicator. I can't have you making presentations like that anymore. If you do, I'll have to hire someone who knows how to play ball."

"Message received," I said.

He blinked his left eye rapidly. "Maybe it's a good thing you'll be out of the office for a while. I could use a break."

So could I, I thought.

But I wasn't going to get one.

Marvin was lying helpless in a bed because of me, and I had a vow to keep.

CHAPTER 6

PLEASE HOLD ON. THE TRAIN IS DEPARTING FOR TERMINAL C.

The voice was followed by a chime playing the opening notes of "She'll Be Comin' 'Round the Mountain." I steadied my rolling suitcase with one hand and grabbed the stainless-steel pole with the other. It reminded me of the New York subway, but without the feeling that I'd just contracted hepatitis and was on my way to the emergency room.

I'd ridden the Denver International Airport underground train at least half a dozen times and knew the drill. Hang onto the pole as the car accelerated, watch the pinwheels in the tunnel spin, wonder why the pinwheels were there in the first place, listen carefully to the precious little choo-choo sounds and directions, and try to avoid touching anybody who might take offense.

I rented a forest green Chevy Cruze, the cheapest car I could find. I was on a budget now, no keeping receipts or filling out expense reports. No GPS, either, which I didn't mind, having found myself at odds with the dashboard tyrants who ruled their cars and the drivers thereof.

Exiting the airport, I passed a mammoth blue statue of a frenzied stallion, mane wild and eyes glowing like cigarettes in the dark. A warning that this was the point of no return, maybe. I'd never ventured past the Mile-High City in Colorado, and from here on was uncharted territory.

The sky was clear, almost indigo. Keeping an eye on the Rockies in the west, I drove south on I-25, then southwest. The dry plains began to sprout evergreens and aspen, the latter still thriving despite the recent passage of Labor Day. I could see yellows and oranges on the hillsides as we ascended, promising more to come.

The Cruze and I breathed more deeply as the air grew thinner. I watched the elevation numbers on the city limits signs: 6,110 feet, 7,390 feet. Stopping for gas at a Diamond Shamrock station in a town called Tabor, I bought a ham and cheese sandwich and two bottles of water. I could feel the dryness in my nose and throat and wondered about nosebleeds.

Just past Tabor I saw a WELCOME TO CRYSTAL COUNTY sign. I thought of Marvin driving past it, too. How fast had he been going? Was his throat dry? Did he have the radio on, listening to Motown?

The leaves were vivid now, the aspens yellow as peppers and the rest a pumpkin hue. Traffic was heavier than I'd expected, probably tourists following the fall colors. I drove another 50 miles or so. When I tried the radio I got mostly static.

Then I hit the motherlode, or so the sign said.

ENTERING MOTHERLODE
POP. 527
ELEVATION 8,843 feet

There was no sign saying AS SEEN IN THE BOOK *DARKNESS AT DAWN*. But everything had happened here.

The main street started with a public park, a mom-and-pop grocery, a Conoco gas station. From there it was mostly shops and little restaurants. About half the parking spaces were taken. Then came the sheriff's office, and the volunteer fire department with a sign that said LIBRARY on the second floor. Houses were next, a row of tiny Victorian bungalows on each side of the street, painted in pastels with gingerbread trim that made them look like Easter eggs. Last came the motels, the bed-and-breakfasts, none of them large, half of them old and charming and the other half just old.

I drove slowly, one eye on the reservation printout in my hand. I wanted the Lodgepole Inn, the only affordable place I'd been able to find with a vacancy. At last I spotted it, set well back from the road. The sign, its letters shaped like Lincoln Logs, looked like it was marking its 50th anniversary, too.

The Inn was a semicircle of eight log cabins, stained a faded redwood color and chinked with smears of gray cement. I pulled into the gravel lot and parked in front of the first building, the one with the OFFICE sign.

With a grunt I extricated myself from the car, only to find myself slapping my palm on the roof for support. I was lightheaded, no doubt from the altitude.

I stood there long enough to get my bearings. In the distance I saw cliffs, gray and jagged. A single cloud hung over them like a smoke signal.

Taking a deep breath, I crunched my way to the front door. Inside, the desk was made of more Lincoln Logs with a varnished plywood top. A rack of fliers about area attractions sat in front of the desk, with a revolving display of postcards to the left. It was nearly empty.

A doorbell button was screwed to the plywood. BUZZ FOR ASSISTANCE, said a card next to the plywood. I was about to press when a door behind the desk opened.

"Don't push that thing," groused the woman who emerged, a seventyish apparition straight out of the witches' scene in *Macbeth*. Her gray hair was tangled; she wore no makeup or jewelry. She did wear a nubby pink sweater, though, despite the fact that it wasn't cold.

"I have a reservation," I said, handing her the printout.

She glowered at it. Apparently unable to find anything out of order, she took my credit card and charged it. Turning around, she plucked a key that hung from a plywood rack behind her and tossed it on the counter.

I raised an eyebrow. "A real key? I can't remember the last time I didn't get a key card to swipe."

Her eyes narrowed. "You got a problem with that?"

"No, no. I was just—"

"Two things. Got a cell phone?"

"Yes."

"Service here stinks. Sometimes it works, sometimes not."

"Oh."

"You got a laptop?"

"Uh-huh."

"The wi-fi is crap, too. Good luck with that. Password is Spike. Name of a dog I used to have. He's dead."

"I'm . . . sorry to hear that."

"Also, been having some trouble with your toilet. Just giving you a heads-up."

"Uh . . . thanks."

"If the key won't work, pull it out about a quarter-inch and wiggle it."

I put it in my pocket. "Anything else?"

"Yeah. Have a nice stay."

"Don't know how I could do otherwise," I said, and headed out the door.

* * *

The key to Cabin Six worked without wiggling. Opening the door filled my nose with the smells of bleach and burnt popcorn.

I sat on the bed, a double with a thin mattress. I could feel the springs, but only in the center. Maybe there was a work-around. I'd try later.

The décor was minimal, logs being so interesting on their own. A rusty crosscut saw with wooden handles spanned the back wall like a dreary rainbow. An Indian-style blanket, looking as if it belonged in a more southwestern state, was nailed next to the only window.

I checked my watch. Not quite 2:30. There would be time later to explore the wonders of my new home. I needed to find the sheriff's office, having no idea where else to start.

Taking out my notepad, I proceeded to find the 50-year-old address copied from Marvin's files. But why try to locate the place? I'd just ask the Cranky Old Woman.

This time I hit the buzzer before she could stop me. As a result, she looked even crankier when she came out.

"Complaints already?"

I shook my head. "Can you tell me where the sheriff's office is?"

"Why?"

"I'm trying to find some records they might have."

"About what?"

I took a deep breath and let it out slowly. "About a

murder that took place in this town about fifty years ago. The MacIlhenny case."

She folded her arms. "You a cop or something?"

"I'm working on a book about it."

"A *book*?" She swore under her breath, but not very far under. "Another one? This town's got enough problems. We don't need more bad publicity."

"Could be good for business. Get people's attention."

"Don't want that kind of attention."

I tapped my fingers on the counter. "Never mind. I'll find the sheriff's office myself."

She grunted. "Out of the parking lot, take a left, then a right. Next to the County Courthouse."

"Thanks."

"You owe me one."

"I won't forget," I said, and wiped it from my memory.

* * *

The office was a storefront the size of a frontier saloon, with CRYSTAL COUNTY SHERIFF on the window in 1880s Gold Rush type. Apparently it had moved sometime during the last half century, but only down the street.

The dispatcher, a woman with a headset and a hint of a mustache, looked up when I came in. A black microphone and a stack of audio equipment sat on the desk in front of her.

"Help you?"

"Is the sheriff in?"

"I think he's on the phone." She nodded over her shoulder at the desk behind her, where sat a thirtyish, mocha-skinned man with a khaki uniform and a sleek, black ponytail. He was filling out some kind of report. "Maybe the deputy can help you."

The man put down his pen. "Yes, ma'am."

After introducing myself, I told him what I was looking for.

He pushed back from his desk. "Before my time. Before the sheriff's time, too, but maybe he knows something about the records. Guess you'll need to talk to him."

The dispatcher checked the lights on her landline. "He's still on the phone."

"I'll wait," I said, and sat in one of three chairs near the door.

The room had five desks, two of them unoccupied. In the back on the left was a door, presumably to the sheriff's inner sanctum; to the right was an empty jail cell. I expected the latter to look like something from Dodge City, with rounded iron bars and a cot chained to the wall, but it was all new steel and plastic.

The dispatcher checked her lights again, then picked up her phone. "Have a lady here with questions about records from fifty years ago. A murder case. Thought you might know." She paused. "I'll send her in."

The nameplate on the door said SHERIFF WOODY TANAKA. Inside, he was looking at a grainy faxed photo, probably from a wanted poster. He motioned me toward the chair across from him. "One second," he said, reading.

I sat. It could have been a high school principal's office. A gallery of framed photos, presumably his wife and kids, surrounded his computer monitor. He looked to be in his late forties, medium build, Japanese-American.

"So, you're interested in records." He looked up, his expression earnest.

Once again I introduced myself and explained what I was looking for. I was starting to think I should have it printed on fliers I could hand out.

He sat there for a moment. "Your friend Marvin came looking for me a couple months ago." He shook his head. "I can show you what I showed him."

He got up and pulled a folder from one of the file cabinets behind him. "Never heard of this case before I got here, and that was just over two years ago. Put in six years as a deputy in Denver. So, I don't want to knock one of my predecessors. But Sheriff Boyle doesn't seem to have been big on record-keeping. There's hardly anything in the file."

He dumped the contents on his desk. "Looks like he did a few interviews with family and friends of Iris MacIlhenny, Gant, and people who knew Skye, the hippie guy. Made a little list of people he thought might be fellow drug users. There's one blurry group photo with Skye in it. If there was any physical evidence, it's been lost."

I glanced through what was there. "I've seen most of this in Marvin's files from the original book. When you saw him, did he say who else in town he was talking to?"

"No, I think I was the first. I sent him to Art Keebler."

"Who?"

"He puts together a magazine. Maybe you've seen it in racks around town. *Motherlode Monthly*. Mostly a collection of ads. But he writes articles about the town's history, too, kind of filler around the ads. The guy's a walking historical encyclopedia."

"Where can I find him?"

"Got a little office down the street. Understand he spends a lot of time at the Historical Museum, too."

I stood up. "I'll try there. Thanks for your time."

He replaced the papers in the folder. "God knows we've got plenty to do, but this case kind of intrigues me. This county hasn't had a really interesting one in years. So I'll do whatever I can to—"

There were three sharp raps on the door, and it opened. The dispatcher stuck her head in. "Lloyd called. Half a dozen tourists smoking pot in Patriots' Park. He'd like backup."

Tanaka looked at me. "See what I mean?"

The file drawer rolled shut with a *thunk*. "Talk to Art. You need anything else from me, let me know."

* * *

The *Motherlode Monthly* office was the size of a public restroom. It was also closed.

A note was taped to the door:

GONE TO HISTORICAL MUSEUM, BACK 4 P.M.

I drove around looking for the museum, finally finding it in what looked like a converted train station. It was a museum piece itself, white paint turned chalky, weathered shake roof dipping slightly in the middle. Crisscrossed rebar had been added to the windows, as if the place housed something valuable, which perhaps it did.

A car with Nebraska license plates had parked in front, as did I. An older couple got out, tried the doorknob, peered inside, then drove away. I found a note taped to the door:

GONE TO MOTHERLODE MONTHLY OFFICE, BACK 10 A.M.

I felt like the rube in a shell game.

Retracing my steps to the office, I saw an ancient green Jeep parked in front. I was relieved to find Keebler at his desk, talking on the phone. A gangly man with a white fringe of hair and a hatchet nose, he pointed at me to acknowledge my presence but kept talking.

"Rudy," he said, his voice a little hoarse, "they say it takes money to make money. I believe it. No offense, but your ad's no bigger than a business card. A plumber needs at least a half page. Graphics. You should have a faucet. A smiling faucet. Something about 24-hour emergency service."

He paused, rubbing his forehead with the heel of his palm. "I'm in the same boat, man. If we don't extend ourselves a little—"

I could hear the voice at the other end, but couldn't tell what it was saying.

"Okay," Keebler added. He blinked hard, as if trying to get something out of his eye. "I'll touch base with you in a month. If you're still in business."

Hanging up, he shook his head. "No sense of community."

He looked me over, but not in that #MeToo way I sometimes encountered. "Have a seat. Don't recognize you, so you must not be here to tell me I misspelled your name or scrambled the phone number in your ad."

"No, the sheriff recommended you. If you've got a few minutes, I have some questions about the town's history."

"You should go to the Historical Museum."

"I was just there. Nobody else was."

He massaged his temples with two fingers. "Yeah, I have to split my time. The magazine doesn't pay much anymore, and the museum's all volunteer. But history's still my thing."

"That's what I heard."

He got to his feet. "You have something to take notes with?"

I took out my pad and pen and held them up.

"I've got a presentation on this subject. I update it every year. I've given it at the museum, American Legion, Founder's Day, probably twenty or thirty schools. Anybody who'll listen. You want the extremely condensed version?"

"I'm ready."

He cleared his throat, then started pacing. "Motherlode's past is as colorful as its sunsets. It was incorporated in 1888, two years after the discovery of gold by prospector Edgar Auchincloss. In a single year the population ballooned from two-fifty to twelve thousand."

"Huh," I said, but wasn't taking notes yet.

"The town was notorious for its saloons, gambling, and brothels." He paused. "I leave out the brothels for the school kids," he confided, then continued.

"It was also known for its corrupt politicians. Worst of all was its second mayor, Colonel Albert 'Cannonball' Dunigan, a former Civil War officer whose rivals would simply disappear. But his largesse was legendary, and the Free Whiskey Tuesdays he imposed on the taverns kept him in office for three terms."

He put his hands in his pockets. "Crusading newspaperman Harold P. Trayne of the *Crystal County Gazette* finally put an end to Dunigan's reign with a series of articles. But not before losing one arm, a leg, and the hearing in his right ear under suspicious circumstances."

I nodded, wondering whether I should ask him to skip to the murder. But he seemed to be in a sort of trance.

"In 1912, Edgar Auchincloss sold the Victory Mine to Joshua Gant, who became one of Colorado's first millionaires. Gant left it to his son, Franklin, whose greatest act of philanthropy was funding the Motherlode Historical Society and Museum. Unfortunately, by the time Franklin died in

1997, the mine was played out. And in many ways, so was Motherlode."

I started taking notes, mostly for show.

"People, especially families, started moving away. The schools closed, and the few remaining young people were home-schooled or bused to Copper Ridge, thirty miles away. The year-round population fell to about five hundred, swelling to sixteen hundred in the summer."

He seemed pleased that I was writing and began building to a big finish. "But the spirit of Motherlode lives on. Today the world comes to see our rugged volcanic cliffs, our fiery groves of aspen, our charming shops and galleries and restaurants. And the town may well be on the verge of a renaissance. Franklin Gant's son, Troy, has plans to reopen the Victory Mine as a source of molybdenum, a mineral vital to the production of steel, petroleum, electrical filaments, missiles, and aircraft."

He paused. "Any questions?"

"Actually, I was wondering about something else."

"Demographics? Ninety-two percent Caucasian, two percent Native American, four percent Hispanic. Median household income thirty-four thousand dollars. Median age forty-six; twenty percent sixty-five or older."

"Well, I—"

"Weather? In summer, average high about seventy, low forty. Winter, high of freezing with low of zero. Annual snowfall around a hundred and fifty inches."

"A hundred and fifty? That's . . . more than ten feet."

He nodded. "Another reason folks find it hard to live here. As for politics, slightly more Democrats than Republicans, with surprisingly few independents. Economy: About seventy percent tourism and retail—"

I raised a palm, trying to stop him. "What I really need is a little different."

He sat down, looking a bit winded. "Such as?"

"I'm trying to find out about the MacIlhenny murder."

He frowned. "This isn't about a book, is it?"

"Well, yes."

He shook his head. "Another man came through here a while back. Sheriff sent him to me, too. Any connection?"

I told him about Marvin.

He sighed. "Too bad about your friend. But as I told him, he probably knows more about it than I do. That's true of most people here. It's ancient history."

"I thought history was your thing."

"So's business. You heard me talking on the phone, right?"

"Loud and clear."

"Colorado's full of ghost towns that boomed and died, especially mining towns. The state doesn't have half the tourism budget it needs, and neither do we. Got to project a positive, family-friendly image."

"Then why talk about Colonel What's-his-name and a reporter who lost his leg?"

"Because that's *really* ancient history. Colorful, like pirates and the *Titanic*. The MacIlhenny murder is too real, too tragic."

I put the pad and pen back in my pocket. "Okay. Thanks for the presentation."

"Sorry I can't help you."

I stood, then suddenly lost my balance and dropped back into my chair. Points of light danced before my eyes, and I had the urge to put my head down.

"You need to drink more water," Keebler said matter-of-factly. "Don't want to get altitude sickness. Your friend had the same problem. Takes a while to get acclimated."

"I'll remember that."

Slowly I tried standing again. My head was only half-empty this time, and the room no longer spun.

I made my way to the door and into the sunshine. *Get water,* I thought.

Oh, and one more thing.

Cross Mr. Keebler off the helpful list and put him on the other one.

CHAPTER 7

Armed with two bottles of water from the Conoco station, I went on a drinking binge in the Cruze. Fortunately, the station also featured restrooms.

I returned to my Lincoln Log cabin, trying to decide where to go for dinner. I dared not ask the Cranky Old Woman, who clearly wanted me to suffer food poisoning as soon as possible. Instead I consulted the reviews on Yelp.

The three-star winner in the budget-conscious category was the Ore Cart Café, which proved to be a tiny place downtown between the Assay Tavern and the Claim Jumper Gallery. There was an actual ore cart just inside the front door, and a bear in the corner, a feat of taxidermy that seemed to loom over everything else.

I had the Forty Karat Pasta, which was much easier to chew than it sounded, along with as much ice water as I could hold. After two more visits to the restroom, I decided altitude sickness might not be so bad after all.

Back at the Lodgepole Inn, I retired for the night. It turned out that the only workaround for the thin mattress and intrusive springs was to expect as little sleep as possible.

The toilet I'd been warned about didn't overflow, but hissed and gurgled until morning.

* * *

It was in a diminished state that I gathered my notes soon after dawn and returned to the Ore Cart for breakfast. I ordered the specialty of the house, Gold Strike Flapjacks, which were just regular pancakes with butterscotch chips and honey. Dr. Garabedian had urged me once to eat as many brightly colored foods as possible for the antioxidants, so I was sure he would have approved.

My jaw worked as I went over all I'd underlined in Marvin's book, copied from his files, and heard during my visits to the sheriff and the recalcitrant Mr. Keebler. What was next?

I couldn't interview the dead. Or Skye, the missing flower child. Had any of the principals survived the last 50 years, preferably within driving distance?

There was Gant's son, Troy, the one with dreams of reopening the mine. But according to Marvin's book, he'd been a preschooler at the time. That left one possibility: Iris MacIlhenny's little sister, Rose. Fifty years ago, she'd been 14.

I wondered what it had been like to lose a sister. To grow up knowing how notoriously she'd died, with her name in the newspapers and on television and in a book.

Could Rose still be alive? If so, had she moved away?

I took out my phone to look her up. NO SERVICE, the screen said.

I set the phone down and kept chewing. A few moments later the waitress, a woman who faintly resembled the bear in the corner but with an apron and a much sunnier disposition, came by. "More coffee?" she asked, brandishing an old-fashioned glass decanter.

"Yes. Thanks."

As she poured, I watched the steam rise. "How long have you lived here?" I asked.

"About four years."

"Heard of Rose MacIlhenny?"

She stopped pouring. "Sure."

"Any idea whether she's still around?"

"Oh, yeah. Got a gift shop, other side of town."

"You're kidding." I paused. "You know about her sister?"

"Didn't know she had one."

I raised an eyebrow. Ancient history, Keebler had said. Perhaps he was right about something.

A few minutes later I paid at the register, then got directions to the shop.

On the way out, I asked myself why anyone would stay nearly 50 years in a town full of such corrosive memories.

Maybe I was about to find out.

* * *

The place was called Simply Rose. I was taken aback, having assumed that Motherlode business names were required to sound like minerals, not animals or vegetables.

A dozen or so customers meandered in the aisles—mostly women, plus two domesticated males who trailed their significant others with eyes glazed. The scent of roses tinged the air, not the aerosol counterfeit but the real item. Behind the register on a stool sat a teenage boy, brown hair dangling in his eyes, wearing a COPPER RIDGE ROCKERS sweatshirt. He was reading what looked like a graphic novel, perhaps my least favorite literary form, occasionally pausing to ring up a purchase.

I looked around for anyone who might be Rose. Before long I spied a likely candidate talking with a female customer. Something about the way she seemed to own the place told me she was Rose. That and the fact that she wore the only pale pink business suit I'd ever seen.

If she was 64, it didn't show. She was tall, trim, a bit square-jawed. Her cheekbones were high, her champagne hair gathered in a chignon style.

I waited. But her customer's supply of questions seemed bottomless, so I rambled through the store. The shelves were neatly stocked with a little of everything, much of it rose-themed—bath salts, chocolates, silk flowers, cologne, hand towels, soaps, even a soup mix I wasn't eager to try. The rest was mostly geological—geodes, crystals, gold-plated aspen leaf earrings, rock tables, marble bookends, paperweights, fossils.

Eventually it was my turn. "Excuse me," I said. "I'm looking for any reading material you might have about this area."

She smiled. "Right this way." Leading me toward the counter, she left the fragrance of roses even stronger in her wake.

At a revolving rack she stopped. It was laden with booklets, most of their covers displaying old sepia-toned photos and the same Gold Rush type I'd seen in the sheriff's window. Self-published or a small regional press, I figured.

She pulled one from the top row. "They're not all about this particular town, of course, or even Crystal County. But they're all on Colorado. This one's about Motherlode."

She handed it to me. *The Town that Was a Treasure,* it said. The author was one Arthur Keebler.

Somehow I wasn't surprised.

"Is this the kind of thing you mean?" she asked.

"Exactly. As a matter of fact, I was speaking with this gentleman yesterday."

"Ah. Then you know he's quite the expert."

"So he told me."

She burst out laughing. "Oh," she said, as if saying more might get her into trouble.

I picked up the slender volume and leafed through it, not really paying attention to what was on its pages. "Actually, I'm working on a book myself about the town's history. One event in particular."

"Really. And what would that be?"

I returned the booklet to the rack. "One I wish had never happened. Involving your sister, Iris."

Her smile faded. "I see." She looked around at the other customers, doubtless preferring to talk with anyone who only wanted to know the price of potpourri.

"My apologies," I said. "I know you have work to do. But maybe we can talk when you have time."

She shrugged. "It's . . . all right. Just been a long time since anyone asked me about those days."

I extended my hand. "Carolyn Neville. I work for Pendleton House Publishing."

She shook it. "Apparently, you know who *I* am."

"Have you read *Darkness at Dawn*?"

She hesitated. "For a long time I wasn't ready to. Waited until I was out of college. Even then I had to skip some parts."

"I'm sure."

"Maybe it was well done, but I couldn't be objective about it."

"Of course not." I paused. "We're trying to update the book. Hoping to shed some new light. Maybe even find out what really happened."

She looked away. "Nobody's been able to do that in fifty years."

"We think there's new information to be had. New ways

to analyze it. The author was just getting started when someone put him in the hospital. He's in a coma."

"My God, that's terrible."

"So I'm picking up where he left off."

She shook her head. "You really think you can figure out who killed Iris?"

"Only if we get the help of people like you. *Especially* you."

"I'm not sure I have anything to say that hasn't been said a thousand times."

"Well, let's find out."

"And I was only fourteen. Thinking about boys and school. You should talk to somebody old enough to know what was going on in this town."

"Any suggestions?"

She turned away from the counter. "There. See those two rock tables?"

I looked where she was pointing. They were coffee tables, their frames dark-stained wood and their tops some kind of thick, clear resin. Floating in the resin were fist-sized slices of agate, some like caramel, some like grape, all translucent and lit from underneath. They weren't the sort of furniture I wanted at home, but to each his own.

"Very nice," I said.

"They're made by a man who lives right here in town, George Svoboda. Must be at least ninety now. Oldest person in Motherlode, as far as I know."

"And I should talk to him?"

"He was here when it happened. Didn't exactly know him then, but I remember him. He worked in the mine."

"I'll talk to him."

"His house is on Cavern Street. Eight-twelve. Go west about two miles."

I nodded. "And I need to talk to you, too." I fished a business card from my purse and gave it to her. "Please call me when it's convenient."

"I don't want to get my hopes up. But if there's really a chance . . ." She left the rest unspoken and stuck the card in her pocket. "I'll call, I promise. But I'd better get back to work. Nice to meet you."

"My pleasure."

By the time I reached the sidewalk the smell of roses was no more.

Huh, I thought. Maybe information wasn't the only thing I'd find in Motherlode. Mikki Flaherty was 2,000 miles away. I could use a friend here, too.

* * *

Back in the car, I glanced at the passenger seat. Topping the stack of papers was Marvin's book, back cover up, the face in his photo looking impossibly young.

I remembered how he'd looked in the hospital, ashen and still. Was he any better? Worse?

And Tracy. Was she sitting in the purple chair next to her husband's bed, trying to ignore the monitor and waiting for another doctor to stick his head in and shrug and tell her nothing had changed?

I dialed her number. This time the call went through, but only to voice mail. Leaving a message seemed like the right thing to do, but I didn't know what to say and hung up.

I started the car. What was next? If Marvin were here, what would he do? What had he already done? So far I knew he'd talked to the sheriff and Keebler, but apparently not Rose. If he'd discovered something earthshaking, I couldn't guess what it was.

What was that name, the one Rose had told me? George Svoboda? Cavern Street? I'd try him.

At this point I'd try anything.

* * *

Cavern Street was past the Victorian cottages, out where things started to fall apart. The ramshackle stage hadn't been reached, but the yellow grass was taller, weedier. Vehicles were more likely to be rusty, tireless, and stranded on concrete blocks.

I watched for 812, but house numbers were spotty. After about five minutes I glimpsed SVOBODA on a mailbox, the name carefully lettered in black paint but nearly weathered off. The compact house was apple green, in better shape than some of its neighbors. The porch pillars were encased in cement, with chunks of rock pressed into it like raisins.

No one answered the door. But I could hear something screeching in the back yard, probably an electric saw.

I walked toward the racket, rounding the corner. There, his back to me, a short, stocky figure in washed-out blue overalls hunched over a circular saw. A broad-brimmed straw hat covered his head.

Circling in front of him, I waited. The old man kept his eyes on the blade, a loaf of rock in his leather gloves. Goggles shielded his glasses. His movements were so slow I thought he might be making his last piece of furniture.

Finally the saw whined to a stop. He straightened, but not much. After coughing for a disturbingly long time, he saw me and pulled off the goggles.

"Mr. Svoboda?" I said.

He turned his head slightly to the side. "What did you say?"

"Hello!"

He took off his hat and wiped his forehead with the back of his hand. His hair was still gray but thin, his eyebrows so dark and thick they made him look angry. At least I hoped it was the eyebrows.

I introduced myself. "I was just looking at one of your tables. In Rose MacIlhenny's store."

"Yes, Rose," he said. "A sweet girl. You are looking for a customized piece, maybe?"

I couldn't place the accent. Eastern European. Czech, maybe.

"Well, no," I said. "According to Rose, you can tell me what this town was like fifty years ago."

He pulled his hat back on. "This is what happens when you don't die soon enough. Everybody asks you about the old days. You want to know about the Victory Mine?"

"Actually, I have some questions about what happened to Rose's sister, Iris."

He raised his formidable brows. "This is suddenly a big subject again? Everybody wants to know."

"Everybody?"

"About a month ago a man was here. Black man. He wrote that book nobody wants to talk about. Keebler, the one from the magazine, sent him to me."

I shook my head. Marvin had been busy, all right. I told the old man what had happened to him.

"This is the kind of world we live in. A world of beasts."

"What did you tell my friend, exactly?"

He shrugged. "At my age, how much could I remember?"

"You seem pretty sharp to me."

He put his hat back on. "I told him about Iris. A lovely young lady. People put her on a pedestal. She wasn't as perfect as they made her out to be, but she loved her students."

"Marvin believed Franklin Gant killed her. What do you think?"

He took off his gloves, then slowly flexed his fingers. The

joints looked swollen. "I worked for him at the Victory mine. From blaster to brakeman, twenty-seven years. He was a rich man, no patience with laziness. Loved his rifles, his dogs. We didn't like him, and he didn't understand us. But I never saw him throttle anyone. And the pay was good for those days."

"What about Sheriff Boyle?"

"A law and order man. Also a ladies' man, if you ask me. Always won the election."

"He blamed the murder on a young man who called himself Skye. Do you remember Skye?"

He put his gloves back on. "The drug boy. Not here long. I would see him at the Pick and Shovel. Barely held a job cleaning the tables. All I know was that he smiled too much. Smelled like incense. Quoted a lot of stupid hippie poetry by some *komunisticka* he called a prophet."

He made a fist and started coughing into it, a loud hacking that made my own chest hurt. It took him almost half a minute to recover.

"What comes of working the mines," he said, his voice frayed. "Thank God it wasn't coal."

"I hear Gant's son wants to reopen the mine."

He shook his head. "Troy Gant knows nothing about mining."

"You don't think it'll work?"

"I say only it is a good thing his father died before seeing how his son turned out." He held up two fingers and made a snipping motion. "They were not cut from the same cloth."

"They must have been upset by my friend's book."

He shrugged again. "Maybe."

"Perhaps Gant is angry at my friend for hurting his father's reputation. How far do you think he'd go to defend it? Would he attack my friend?"

The old man grunted. "Gant Junior cares only for himself.

On the other hand, he would do anything to open that mine again."

There was silence. I tried to think of something else to ask but couldn't.

"Mr. Svoboda, you've been a big help."

He nodded. "I hope your friend wakes up."

He turned to a workbench on his right. Another machine sat on it, something with a revolving red steel drum. He shut it down, unscrewed the canister, and pulled out a stone. It was the size of a golf ball but flatter, clear and wet and shiny, with black veins running through it like scribbles.

"Tourmalated quartz," he said. "Some people think it brings good luck, but of course they're full of *posetilost.*"

I raised my eyebrows, which were no match for his.

"*Posetilost.* It's not what you think. It means foolishness."

He handed me the rock. "Keep it for your friend. And yourself."

"Thanks." I dropped it into my pocket, then turned to go.

"You are sure you don't want a table?" he asked.

"I'll think about it."

"Don't think too long. I'm not getting any younger."

I sighed. Neither was I.

I couldn't stay in this town forever. Couldn't afford it. And I was supposed to make up for lost time, not fall further behind.

I had to find somebody who could tell me something I didn't know.

In this case, it was someone who probably hated Marvin, hated his book, and was about to start hating me.

Troy Gant.

CHAPTER 8

I'D NEVER BEEN TO A MINE BEFORE, HAVING GROWN UP IN Idaho, where the only things worth digging for were sugar beets.

The Victory Mine was easy to find the next morning, though, thanks to the faded billboards that said TAKE THE TOUR and PAN FOR GOLD and TOUCH HISTORY. About two miles from my lodgings the paved road eroded to gravel. Sunlight flashed through the trees, the yellows and oranges just past their prime, starting to brown.

I parked the car in the empty lot, in front of the chain link fence. Nothing moved but aspen leaves. Their shivering rattle was the only sound.

The gate was open, but just a few inches. I glanced at my watch. Unless Gant kept banker's hours he'd be in that office, the red brick cube with the tile roof. A shiny black SUV sat outside the office. His, I assumed.

NO TRESPASSING, said the sign on the gate. Beyond it I could see the remains of the mine's heyday, a shuttered gift shop and boarded-up concession stand. If he wanted to reopen this place, he had his work cut out for him.

The gate creaked when I pushed it a little farther, my breakfast of Gold Strike Flapjacks not allowing me to squeeze through the gap without adjustment.

No one was inside the building, but the door was ajar.

Suddenly I heard a crash from behind the building, and a muttered curse. Moments later a man appeared, dragging a piece of dented sheet metal.

He seemed out of place. His dark blue polo shirt and jeans were designer grade, his wraparound sunglasses vaguely European. Paunchy but not fat, he looked about 55. His top-heavy frame was a duplicate of Franklin Gant's, but the unnatural auburn hair and tan were completely his own.

He dropped his jaw and the sheet metal in surprise, but quickly recovered. "Hey!" he said, grinning. "What can I do you for?" There was something in his eye and tone that made me think about the pepper spray in my purse.

I introduced myself. "I wonder if I could ask you a few questions."

He waved toward the door. "If you got the money, Honey, I got the time."

Inside the office he slipped off his sunglasses and set them on his desk next to a laptop. Maps and architectural renderings plastered the walls. A smaller desk was in the corner, unoccupied.

"A publisher, huh?" he said, sitting down. "Don't think I ever met one of those before."

I lowered myself into the chair across from him. "And I've never met a man who wants to bring a gold mine back from the dead."

He stuck a finger in his ear and wiggled it. "Yeah, well, she's not dead yet. We're gonna rise again."

He pointed at one of the drawings on the wall, a visitor's center with a crowd of blank-faced humanoids milling around the entrance. "See that? We're estimating a quarter million tourists a year. Heck, Breckenridge gets a million and half. Even Copper Ridge has almost half a mil."

I made an interested noise.

"We'll have a new entrance, gift shop, snack bar. Tours, of course. Maybe even a zip line, some kiddie rides. Besides, gold's not the only game in town. I don't know if you're aware of this, but molybdenum is the unsung metal of the twenty-first century."

"You don't say."

"'Course there's a lot of government red tape involved. Colorado Division of Reclamation, Mining and Safety alone wants you to fill out enough forms to kill an acre of trees." He pointed at the empty desk in the corner. "I've still got two employees—night guard and half-time secretary. It's only a matter of time."

It sounded like the agency Gant loved most was the Department of Wishful Thinking.

There followed an awkward silence.

"Well, enough of that," he said. "You had some questions?"

"About the Iris MacIlhenny killing."

He groaned. "You're kidding. I thought that old story had been put to rest."

I shook my head, then told him about the new edition and what had happened to Marvin.

Unlike the sheriff and Rose and Mr. Svoboda, Gant skipped the condolences. "My dad had nothing to do with that girl," he said.

"Contrary to what the book says."

"That's right. My father was a strong, successful businessman, not a crazy strangler. He took the mine and made it an economic engine for this town and the county. Some people are just jealous."

"So who do *you* think killed Iris?"

"I was only five when it happened. How should I know?"

"But you must have heard plenty about it while you were growing up. From your parents."

He shook his head. "They never talked about it. Just kept going, mostly for the town's sake. Now, say they fell apart or moved away. Where would that leave everybody who depended on the mine?"

"You never heard *anything* about the murder?"

"Sure, from kids at school. They'd pick up crap from *their* parents, then get it all mixed up and use it to make fun of me. You know how kids are."

I nodded. I couldn't help knowing how children are, having grown up more interested in Carl Sandburg than Carl Yastrzemski. But there was no need to bring that up.

"You don't even have a *theory* about who killed Iris?" I asked.

He shrugged. "Maybe the old sheriff was right. Could have been that drug addict, Skye. I don't think anybody will ever know."

He looked at me. I looked at him.

"Anything else I can help you with?" he asked.

"Maybe down the road."

I got up to leave; he did the same.

"My door's always open," he said. "Except when I'm in Denver, trying to talk sense into the bureaucrats."

I gave him my business card. He looked it over, then lowered his voice. "I don't suppose with all your high-powered contacts back there in New York, you know anybody who'd like to invest in the opportunity of a lifetime."

"Afraid not."

He nodded. "That's what they all say. But no worries. I only have to find five or six brave souls who can see past the ends of their noses. They're out there."

Taking me by the elbow with a familiarity that made me want to press charges for something, he ushered me to the door. "You're welcome anytime. Hope you find the real killer. You'd be doing my family a big favor. Defending our honor."

I believed it. As much as anything else he said.

Which was not at all.

* * *

I waited until I reached the city limits before trying to call Stephen for an update. I wanted to try Tracy again, too.

NO SERVICE, said my phone.

Maybe it would help if I got closer to a cell tower, assuming there was one. Not knowing who to ask, I decided to stop at the next building where I'd made at least one acquaintance.

It happened to be Simply Rose.

Business wasn't as brisk this time. The teenage reader of graphic novels was nowhere to be seen. Rose stood at the counter, taking a return from an irate woman who was talking about craftsmanship in America and how there wasn't any. When they'd reached an amicable settlement, I approached her.

Instead of yesterday's pale pink business suit, she wore a white blouse and mint green skirt. She still smelled like a rose garden.

"Carolyn," she said, smiling and looking up from the paperwork she was filling out. "I haven't had a chance to consider our conversation yesterday. So if you're wanting to talk about—"

"No, it's not that. I'm having a problem with cell phone reception."

She looked up, relieved. "Oh, that happens all the time here."

"I wondered whether it makes a difference if you're close to a tower."

She shook her head. "Not that I've noticed. But if you want to try, it's near the Lodgepole Inn, disguised as a very unconvincing tree."

"Lodgepole Inn? I'm staying there."

She looked pained. "Really?"

"It's not so bad. I feel like young Abraham Lincoln, reading his books by candlelight."

She smirked. "I'm sure there's a reason you chose that motel, but you have my sympathies."

My stomach happened to growl at that moment. I took it as divine counsel, sort of.

"I don't want to rush you, but I'd really like to talk. We should go to dinner sometime. I've been eating every meal at the Ore Cart, so I could use a change of pace."

She put down her pen. "Fair enough. My favorite place is *Le Coeur D'Or*. It's pretty fancy, though."

"The Heart of Gold. That's about as far as my high school French goes. What night works for you?"

"I think they're about to close for the winter, so you'd better hurry."

I checked my watch. "When do you close?"

"Tonight? Five-thirty."

"I'll be here at five forty-five."

"Wish I could say I've got a previous engagement, but my social life sucks. I'll look forward to it."

I drove back to the Lodgepole Inn. There, about 300 yards behind the cabins, stood the ersatz tree Rose had mentioned, rising like a giant scrub brush above the others.

Still no bars.

I put the phone away. It was lonely here on the dark side of the moon. I was really looking forward to dinner now.

* * *

The Heart of Gold was indeed sophisticated. I could tell because the menu was in French, the waiter wore a black vest and purple cummerbund, and there were no dead animals in the corner.

Our reservations were for 6:15. I'd had no trouble getting them, other than driving there to make them, my phone currently being as useful as last year's desk calendar.

The décor was mostly red velvet and fake gaslights, dim enough to hide a multitude of janitorial sins. The atmosphere was hushed, mainly because we were the only customers at the dozen or so tables.

"Have you been here before?" I asked Rose when we were seated.

"Oh, yes, a few times. Charlie and I used to come here."

"Charlie?"

She studied the menu. "We were engaged at one point. Didn't work out. He moved to Boulder."

"Sorry to hear that."

She shrugged. "It happens."

"I know. Happened to me twice. Not an engagement, but almost."

She put the menu down. "Men. Can't live with 'em, can't disembowel 'em."

I nodded, but still wished I could find the right one.

She looked around. "I imagine this place doesn't seem all that sophisticated if you work in New York City."

"Manhattan's not all it's cracked up to be. No mountains. No big rocks jutting out of the ground."

"Speaking of rocks, have you talked to George Svoboda yet?"

"Yeah, I went to see him yesterday."

"How did that go?"

"Quite a character, isn't he? Doesn't hesitate to share his opinions about anybody."

"Did he say anything you can use?"

"I'm not sure yet."

The waiter approached. When he suggested a bottle of Cabernet Franc, Rose declared it a fine choice. I started wondering about prices, but didn't want to be too obvious by checking the menu.

"Mr. Svoboda remembers Iris," I said when the waiter was gone. "But I'm sure the two of you have discussed her."

She shook her head. "All we talk about is rock tables. And the weather."

"He said she was wonderful, but not perfect. She loved her students."

"Most people would say the same thing. Except for the part about not being perfect. A lot of people thought she was. And the prettiest girl in town. Which she also was."

"Did she have a boyfriend?"

She looked down at the menu again. "If she did, it wasn't public knowledge. I know your friend's book said Franklin Gant was after her, but that never sounded right to me. She didn't talk about him."

"What *did* she talk about?"

"Not much. Not to me, anyway. We were eleven years apart, so I wasn't her confidant or anything."

The waiter reappeared with our wine, then took our orders. As usual, I chose the least expensive thing I could pronounce. Rose picked the Chicken Basquaise. I wondered whether she'd ordered it before, when she and Charlie were at the height of their doomed romance.

She lifted her goblet. "To Iris."

The glasses clinked. I was no wine expert, but it tasted sort of earthy, with a hint of raspberry. I hoped it was worth the money, whatever that turned out to be.

She set hers down, then gazed at it. "Hard to believe it's been fifty years. She was so popular. Practically everybody came to her funeral. The church couldn't hold them all. Kids from her classes were there, looking so sad and scared."

She took another sip. "Now she's in the cemetery outside of town, next to all those prospectors and politicians and ladies of the evening." She sighed. "My parents never got over it."

"Did you?"

She looked away. "It's been a long time. But probably not. I doubt anybody ever does."

I took a sip of ice water. "Yet you've gone on to have your own business, which I assume is successful. And in the very town where it all happened."

"After college I lived in Spokane for a while. Opened a gift shop. Lots of blue and pink country décor and pineapple signs that said WELCOME FRIENDS, that kind of thing. It did okay. But I missed the mountains. And some of the people. I've never regretted coming back."

She poured herself a little more wine. "You move on, I guess. I did, anyway."

By the time our food came, the bottle was half empty. I was still on my first glass. The more Rose imbibed, the more candid she became.

We were finishing our food when she glanced around as if to make sure no other patrons had entered. "You know," she murmured, "George was right."

I put down my fork. "About what?"

"About Iris. She really wasn't perfect."

"In what way?"

She shook her head. "I can't really say."

"Can't or won't?"

"I've said too much already. Tell me about you."

"But—"

"Maybe you're more fascinating than you realize."

I sighed. "What would you like to know?"

"Just everything. Where'd you grow up?"

"Idaho, where I was considered pretty odd. Now I live in Connecticut, where I'm seen in much the same way."

"How come?"

I tilted my head to one side. "Let's just say that as a child I focused on activities more commonly associated with unusually boring adults."

"And you've had a stellar career, I'm sure."

"I taught for a little while. Since then, mostly editorial positions, ranging from the mildly unrewarding to the intolerable."

She took another drink. "Hobbies?"

"Not exactly. Reading, of course. Mediocre cooking. Movies. Helping out at church."

"I bet you like classical music."

I shook my head. "But I appreciate *a capella* harmony on low volume."

"I'll try to keep my voice down."

By the time the waiter brought the dessert menu, the cabernet was nearly gone. Rose smiled frequently, her complexion starting to match her name. She turned down the opportunity for chocolate mousse, citing fullness. I did the same, but for budgetary reasons.

After paying an alarming bill and undeserved gratuity, I drove her home. Not surprisingly, her house was one of the small and spotless Victorians. The streetlight revealed it was no kind of pink, but at least three shades of green.

"I had a lovely evening," Rose said, climbing out of the car. "See you around."

She went inside, the wind clearing away the last hint of cabernet.

I drove into the darkness.

She'd said too much already?

I'd never figure this out if she didn't say a whole lot more.

CHAPTER 9

NEXT MORNING THE BARS WERE BACK IN CABIN SIX. I COULD call Stephen.

"Carolyn?" he answered. "I've been trying to get hold of you."

I closed my eyes, bracing for the worst.

"It's Hunter. He's making threatening noises again."

"I'm afraid you'll have to be more specific."

"He's saying the revised edition is a waste of time. The sales forecast finally came in, and it's dismal."

"Define *dismal*."

"Seventy-five hundred the first year. All downhill after that. Wouldn't break even for three years, and that's without counting the advance."

I opened my eyes. "Ridiculous."

"Yeah, but Hunter says he'll never convince them otherwise. Not after the presentation you gave at—"

"No need to complete that sentence, thank you."

"He says he wants you back at your desk, working on books that have a chance of selling. I don't know what to tell him."

I thought for a moment. I didn't know either.

"Don't tell him anything," I said. "I'll take care of him."

"How? If it involves tennis balls, I can do it myself."

"Just leave it to me."

He paused. "Have you heard from Tracy? How's Marvin?"

"I haven't been able to reach her."

"What about you? Have you found anything out?"

"A few things. Talked to a lot of people, but no big break so far."

There was a long pause.

"Anything else?"

"I made a new friend. Iris MacIlhenny's sister."

"You're kidding. I didn't know she had one."

"She knows more than she's saying." I paused. "Let me know how things go with Hunter."

"I will. Call me when you know something. Bye."

I tried to call Tracy next, but got only voice mail for the third time.

Finally I called Hunter.

Unfortunately, I reached him on the first try. I told him what Stephen had told me, leaving out the tennis balls.

"There's still time to make this work," I said. "But if we want to finish the project more quickly, I need Stephen's help."

"Absolutely not. When Sales says it can't sell something, it does its best to make that happen. Or not happen. I can't take a chance on a book like that."

Take a chance, I thought. Maybe I needed to do that.

"Are you a gambling man?" I asked.

"Not where books are concerned."

"What if you couldn't lose?"

"But I *would* lose."

"Not if you're guaranteed to win. If the book doesn't sell,

you can fire me. If it does sell, I get a three percent net royalty."

There was a long silence. "Define *sell*," he said.

I took out my notepad and pen and started taking notes.

"Break-even in eighteen months," I said.

"No, a year."

"All right, a year."

"Including the advance."

I hesitated. "I . . . well, okay."

"Initial press run of twelve thousand."

"You're kidding. Sales said seventy-five hundred."

"We're talking about a book that's sold over a million copies."

"Yeah, in the old days." There was a long silence. "Ten thousand. My final offer."

"Ow. But I accept."

"And the company doesn't pay your expenses or Stephen's."

I flinched. I could barely afford my own, much less his.

"Fifty percent of his," I said.

"Twenty-five."

"But—"

"Take it or leave it."

I thought of the check for dinner at *Le Coeur D'Or*. My last supper, so to speak.

"Done," I said, squeezing the word out of my windpipe.

"One more thing," he said. "I don't want to fire you."

"You've *always* wanted to fire me."

"Yeah, but you'd get severance. You have to resign."

"Fine."

"And I want this whole thing in writing."

"I'm sure Our Friends in Legal will be happy to oblige."

"Let's not involve them. This is between you and me. Write a letter of intent."

"I will."

There was a long silence.

"You know, Carolyn," he said, "you're a terrible negotiator."

"All the more reason to get rid of me."

"I like the sound of that," he said, and hung up.

* * *

I felt the adrenaline for about 30 seconds, then wondered what I'd gotten myself into.

I consulted my watch. In 12 minutes the doors of Simply Rose would be open.

Driving to the shop, I wondered whether she'd have anything else to tell me now that she was no longer under the influence.

When I stepped into the shop there were no customers yet. No Rose, either.

Behind the counter sat the same teenage boy with a different graphic novel, this one featuring a giant eyeball against a red background. I didn't want to know the details.

Approaching the register, I told him who I was and offered my hand. He seemed confused for a moment, as if unfamiliar with the traditional method of greeting. Maybe he was so used to texting he'd fallen out of practice. Finally he put down his reading material and managed a fair approximation of a handshake.

"Dax Williams," he said.

"You spend a lot of time here."

He pushed his hair out of his eyes. "Yeah, about fifteen hours a week."

"Mostly after school?"

"Home-schooled. Keep my own hours, right? Mom

thought it would be good, especially after . . . well, never mind."

"But your shirt says Copper Ridge Rockers. Is that a school or a band?"

"Public school. They don't make shirts for homeschoolers. Not that I've seen, anyway."

"Is Rose around?"

"Not this morning. She asked me to cover for her. Sounded kind of sick."

I raised my eyebrows. Food poisoning? A hangover?

"It's happened before," he said. "Probably nothing."

I looked down on his graphic novel, literally and figuratively. "I take it you like those," I said.

"They're okay, I guess."

"Have you ever read a *real* novel?"

"Sure. Mom made me read *Fahrenheit 451.*"

"What did you think?"

He shrugged. "I liked the bonfires. That part was pretty cool." He gave me a triumphant grin, as if to say he had approximately 50 more years to live than I did.

"Have a nice day," I said, and headed out the door.

It was reassuring to know the future of the Republic was in such good hands.

* * *

When Rose answered the door of her green Victorian cottage, her complexion almost matched it.

"Carolyn," she said, sounding as if she'd just gotten out of bed. "Didn't expect to see you here."

She wore jeans and a white sweatshirt. In her hand was a half-empty tumbler of tomato juice. Or a Bloody Mary.

She saw me looking at the glass. "Home remedy. You

probably know what for, and I don't mean deodorizing your dog when he's been sprayed by a skunk. Come on in."

The compact living room was furnished mostly with antiques—hall seat, tufted brown Victorian sofa, two Tiffany-style lamps. No country blue quilts or pineapple signs.

She nodded me toward the couch, then sat at my side. "I'd offer you a drink," she said, lifting her glass. "But you probably don't need it. You were a model of moderation last night. It's my own fault. This wasn't the first time I'd had a little too much to drink."

I sighed. This was getting complicated.

"Carolyn, we haven't known each other for very long. But I've been thinking. There's something I'd like to give you, something I've never let anyone else see. I trust you with it, and I think it's time."

She got up and left the room. I sat there, wondering.

About a minute later she reappeared, carrying something round and pale yellow, about the size of a snare drum. She placed it carefully on the sofa.

It appeared to be an old-fashioned wooden hatbox, secured with a leather strap.

"This belonged to Iris," she said quietly. "I found it in her closet after she passed away. I've never shown it to anybody, not even my parents."

"Should I . . . open it now?" I asked.

"No. Wait until you get back to your cabin. You'll need time to look it over."

"Okay."

"Let me know when you're done. We'll have a lot to talk about."

I nodded, not knowing what to say. I picked it up. It wasn't heavy, probably less than five pounds.

"Please don't tell anyone about this," she said. "Not yet."

"I won't."

I bore it to the front door, where she let me out. Carrying it to the car, I proceeded to set it on the passenger seat. When I tried to put a seatbelt on it, the belt wouldn't fit.

Then I drove away, mystified.

CHAPTER 10

After throwing the deadbolt and closing the curtains of Cabin Six, I laid the hatbox on the bed. Its leather strap was dry, cracked. Carefully I detached it and lifted the lid. A momentary whiff of dust and roses met my nostrils.

Letters, papers, and other memorabilia half-filled the box like a bird's nest. I picked up the first envelope, then remembered: Everything here was potential evidence. My fingerprints were verboten. I had no rubber gloves but didn't want to stop for a trip to the store. I itched to know what Rose had been keeping secret for almost half a century.

I checked my pockets for a handkerchief. Nothing. Heading for the bathroom, I found the spare roll of toilet paper, and wrapped it around my hands like a mummy's.

Slowly I sorted the contents into three piles: envelopes with letters, other documents, and miscellaneous. A small, black beetle lay at the bottom, no doubt dead for decades.

I examined the envelopes. All 13 seemed to have been mailed by the same person to Miss Iris MacIlhenny, no return address.

I pulled the first letter from its envelope and unfolded it.

It was a poem in flowing cursive, no title. Rhyming, iambic pentameter, and rather formal for the 1960s. Clearly the poet hadn't been part of the Robert Frost school, much less a disciple of literary bomb-throwers like Ezra Pound and e.e. cummings:

In all the floral gardens of the world,
I sought the fairest blossom to unfurl.
From Greenland to the Egypt of Osiris,
None could compare with my sweet flower Iris . . .

It continued in that vein for a page and a half, the kind of thing that meant a lot to those involved and nothing to anyone else. At the end were two initials: *D.H.*

Who was D.H.?

Certainly not D.H. Lawrence, who died in 1930 and wasn't known for having such a dainty approach to sex. Maybe Rose had a guess.

I tugged the other 12 odes from their envelopes. They were similar, paying tribute to Iris's smile, tenderness, golden hair, vivacity, intellect, fondness for marzipan, velvet cheeks, lilting voice, and thighs.

I turned to the second pile. It consisted of a single sheet of paper, unevenly trimmed, about five inches by seven.

It was an amateurish, anonymous pencil sketch of a slender young woman with delicate features and light-colored hair, the word IRIS at the top, a small heart at the bottom. I turned it over. The page was blank, save for the word CRY in small type in the lower right-hand corner, cut off after the *y*. The font had a dated look—News Gothic, maybe, popular at the time.

What did CRY mean?

Was it the whole word, or only part? Maybe Rose had suspicions about that, too.

In the third pile were two items. First was a tarnished, silver-plated teaspoon. Its decoration was ornate—crossed pickaxes at the top, the word COLORADO running vertically on the handle, and the image of a skyscraper labeled DANIELS & FISHER TOWER on the bowl.

The second was a matchbook, white and black and sepia. On one side the words BROWN PALACE HOTEL: WHERE THE WORLD REGISTERS circled a map of the globe. On the other was a medieval crest.

The Brown Palace, I knew, was a famous hotel in Denver. Maybe the Daniels & Fisher Tower was there, too. Iris and D.H. could have spent a weekend sightseeing in the Mile-High City. Among other things.

Picking up the drawing, I peered at the word IRIS. Then I compared it to the writing on the envelopes.

I was no handwriting expert, and a one-word sample wasn't much. But they didn't look the same to me.

Had Iris been seeing two men? At the same time?

I remembered Marvin's words on the phone, the last time we'd talked before he was attacked: *People aren't always as they appear.*

And George Svoboda's: *People put Iris on a pedestal. She couldn't have been as perfect as they made her out to be.*

Was this Marvin's secret? That the saintly schoolteacher wasn't really? He couldn't have learned it from the contents of the hatbox, having never seen them, but he might have gathered it from George. The old man was too polite to be specific, but Marvin could have connected the dots.

I looked at the three piles on the bed. Rose was right. I'd need time to make sense of it all. And we *would* have a lot to talk about.

I checked my watch.

An hour from now would do.

* * *

Lunch was a turkey and Swiss sandwich from the convenience store, with a Reese's Peanut Butter Cup for three grams of added protein. I was on a health food kick.

Ten minutes later I was on Rose's front porch, the hatbox under my arm.

When she answered the door, she looked stronger, not green at all. A pink toothbrush was in her hand.

"I was just getting ready to go back to the shop," she said.

"Can you spare a few minutes?"

She looked at the box. "Did you . . ."

"Yes."

She closed the door after me. We sat on the sofa. She was still holding the toothbrush.

"What did you think?" she asked.

"I'm not sure *what* to think. How did you get this?"

She sank back on the couch. "A week or so after Iris died, my parents and I went to her house to sort through her things. I started on the closet off her bedroom. I found the hatbox under a blanket."

"You didn't show it to your parents?"

She shook her head. "As soon as I read one of the letters, I wrapped the box in the blanket and hid it in the trunk of our car. When we got home, I snuck it into my room."

"They *never* saw it?"

"No. I knew it would break their hearts to know their daughter wasn't the angel they'd thought she was."

"That must have been hard for a fourteen-year-old girl to keep secret."

"I could never bring myself to get rid of it. But now my

folks are gone. And you're working on this book. Maybe it's all right for the truth to come out."

"Who do you think D.H. might be?"

"I'm pretty sure it was Dylan Hayes. The art and music teacher. I saw them together a couple of times, walking on a trail behind the school."

"And nobody knew they were having an affair?"

"I guess not."

"You think they visited Denver together?"

"Looks that way."

"How about the picture? Did he draw that?"

She glanced around as if searching for a place to put her toothbrush, then gave up. "I've wondered about that for a long time. Mr. Hayes was an art teacher. You'd think he'd do a little better job with a pencil."

"If he didn't draw it, she must have been seeing someone else, too."

She leaned forward. "The sheriff," she said.

"Boyle?"

"She spent a lot of time after school at his office. Said they were working on an anti-drug program for kids. There were rumors about him being a womanizer, even then. Nobody seemed to care as long as he kept the 'hopheads and anarchists' out of town."

I tapped the hatbox with a finger. "Do you think either of those men could have hurt Iris?"

"I don't know. Mr. Hayes certainly didn't seem like the type. You've read the poems."

"Unfortunately, yes."

"The sheriff? I guess anything's possible. He looked like a pretty strong guy, and when he made speeches about marijuana and protestors he got really wound up."

I placed my palm on the box. "I know you don't want people to know about this yet. But would you mind if I showed it to the current sheriff?"

She looked at the floor for a long moment, then at me. "Just the sheriff, right?"

"Right."

"You get attached to stuff like this," she said sadly. "I guess it's because it's all I have left of her."

"Understandable."

"Okay," she said finally, and stood up. She looked at the toothbrush in her hand as if she couldn't remember how it got there.

"I'll let you go to work," I said.

"Work. Yes. And I'll do the same for you."

I wedged the box back under my arm and made my exit.

I wished Marvin were here to see this.

I wished he were here to see anything.

* * *

Sheriff Tanaka, standing next to the counter, stared at the hatbox. So did the dispatcher. No deputies were present to follow suit.

"Ms. . . . Neville, isn't it?" he asked.

"Could I speak to you in your office?"

He gave a half smile. "Right this way."

The dispatcher frowned, apparently not wanting to be left out.

I followed him in, then closed the door behind me.

He sat on the edge of his desk. "What's that thing under your arm? Looks like a wheel of cheese."

"It's evidence in the MacIlhenny case."

"Well, you've certainly got *my* attention."

After undoing the strap, I lifted the lid. "Do you have any rubber gloves?"

"I believe we do." He went into the next room, rummaged around, and came out with two blue pairs.

I put one on, then picked up a letter. It was so much easier than using toilet paper.

"This is a love poem sent to Iris MacIlhenny by someone with the initials D.H. One of thirteen."

"You're kidding. Where'd you get this?"

"From her sister, Rose."

"She kept it all this time?"

"Without telling a soul. Apparently, Iris was having an affair with D.H. at the time of her death."

"Are you sure? He could have been a stalker, and she was saving the letters to prove it."

I shook my head. "She would have thrown them away."

"Okay, let's say you're right. Who's D.H.?"

"Rose thinks it was another teacher, Dylan Hayes."

He scratched the side of his nose. "I don't think there's a word in the file about him. Was he in your friend's book?"

"No. It's new evidence."

"You think this teacher was the killer?"

"Not necessarily. There's another possibility."

"Who?"

"Sheriff P.J. Boyle."

His eyes narrowed. "That's a pretty serious charge, Ms. Neville. What's your proof?"

I picked up the spoon and matchbook with one hand and the drawing with the other. "Boyle and Iris may have had a tryst in Denver, where Iris got this matchbook and spoon. Boyle may have sketched this picture of her."

"*May* have? Did he sign it?"

"No. That's why I'm here. Do you have anything in the file with Boyle's handwriting on it?"

"I'm sure we do," he said, going to the cabinet and rolling out a drawer. He riffled the folders, plucked a sheet of paper from one of them, and set it on his desk. "A search warrant from his last year in office. Not a great copy, but clear enough."

I placed the drawing next to it. "Let's compare the IRIS to his handwriting."

I bent over the papers. Four characters weren't much to work with. But it seemed to me that the foot of the *R* was similar. And the bottom curve of the *S*.

He came around the desk. "I know what any graphologist will tell you. One word is too small a sample."

"Please try it anyway."

"I'm not a handwriting expert."

"I'm not asking you to testify in court as one. I'd just like your off-the-cuff opinion."

He studied both documents, then shook his head. "Let's just say I can't rule out a match. The *S* is a lot alike."

"And the *R*, I think. So that's a maybe."

"For what it's worth."

I flipped the drawing over. "And what do you think of this?"

He shrugged. "It's blank."

"No, it's not." I picked it up and held it in front of him. "Look closer."

He squinted. "'Cry?'"

"Any idea what that means?"

"Looks like the rest of the word is cut off."

"What starts with 'cry'?"

He stared at the paper. "Something about that looks familiar." He went to the file cabinet again. This time it took longer to find what he was searching for.

"Here," he said finally, rolling the drawer shut and waving an old letter. He set it on the desk.

There it was. CRYSTAL COUNTY SHERIFF'S DEPARTMENT. Same typeface, same size. If someone cut a five-by-seven rectangle from it, he'd get the paper used for the drawing.

"So Ms. MacIlhenny was seeing two men," he said, "maybe at the same time. A love triangle." He paused. "But does that mean one of them strangled Iris? It's just as likely they'd have strangled each other."

"True. But people in love can do strange things."

Sighing, he pulled on the second pair of rubber gloves. "I'll send copies of the artwork and Sheriff Boyle's handwriting to a graphologist the county uses. I can tell you right now she'll say the sample's too small."

I nodded. But sometimes the answers were in the details. Editors sweated the small stuff every day.

On the other hand, sometimes the devil was in the details, too.

CHAPTER 11

Two afternoons later I met Stephen at the Denver airport. When he rose from the depths on the escalator I felt a rush of rightness, a sense that something misaligned had slipped back into place. Somehow it seemed I was home. Or he was.

I raised a hand for attention. He looked tired, but smiled.

When he got close enough to hear, I said the first thing that came to mind.

"Drink lots of water."

"Why?"

"To avoid altitude sickness. But not so much you can't stay out of the bathroom."

"Is that one of the few things you've learned so far?"

"Yes."

"I can see why Hunter's upset."

We headed for short-term parking. "Have you heard from Marvin?" I asked. "From Tracy, I mean? All I get is voice mail."

He sighed. "No change in Marvin. He's been moved to a rehabilitation place, which probably explains why you haven't connected. It's not really rehab in his case. More like a nursing home."

I wanted to stop and kick something but kept walking. "What about Tracy?"

"I think she's burning out. Spends every available minute watching him. Their kids have visited, but they can't stay long."

We took an elevator down, then found the Cruze. "Have the police said anything?"

"About the attack? They don't seem to know anything new, just that he was hit with a piece of pipe or a metal rod."

"Pretty much what I thought. Whoever hit him didn't find the weapon there. Not impulsive, planned. No burglary."

He put his suitcase in the trunk. "I told Tracy I was coming out here. She sends her best."

"She's quite a lady. I promised her I'd keep praying for them every day."

He climbed in. "I'd pray, too, if I thought it would do any good."

"I think it will."

"I guess you missed that study showing people who get prayed for aren't any healthier than the rest of the population. They may even get sicker."

"Prayer's not a vending machine," I said. "Sometimes the answer's no."

"That's a rationalization. You want to have it both—"

"Hold it," I said. "You know what Marvin would say if he were here?"

"What?"

"He'd tell us both to clam up and get to work."

He shrugged. "Probably."

I started the engine.

Yeah, we were both back home.

* * *

With Denver in the rearview mirror, we settled in for a four-hour drive. Stephen took out his phone and started plotting the best stopping points for gas, food, bottled water, and public restrooms.

Around Buena Vista we passed an especially vivid hillside, less browned than the others. Sticking his phone in his pocket, he stared out the window. "Can you believe I've never been to Colorado before? I know we're not here to be tourists, but maybe I can poke around a little."

"Maybe, but we have work to do. And now I'm paying your room and board."

"Then let's get started. What have you got so far?"

I shook my head. "Good thing it's a four-hour drive. Getting you up to speed will take forever."

"I've already read the original book. And the strategy statement."

"We basically have five suspects in the murder. You know about Franklin Gant and Skye the druggie. What you *don't* know is that the sheriff and a schoolteacher could have done it, too."

He raised his eyebrows. "Is that what Marvin was talking about?"

"Possibly." I told him about Rose and the hatbox, and how Marvin had questioned George Svoboda and Art Keebler.

"No wonder somebody hit him."

"We've got two suspects there. Skye, but nobody knows where he is or even if he's alive. And Gant's son, Troy. I've talked to him, too. He seems kind of unlikely."

"Sounds like you've been busy. Too bad Hunter can't see that."

"Fortunately, the current sheriff is on our side."

"Really? You sweet-talked your way into that?"

"No. He's just bored."

He laughed, then looked out the window again. "Anything else I should know?"

"Yeah," I said. "They get ten feet of snow here every year. I hate driving in that stuff."

"It's not even close to winter yet. We'll be out of here long before then."

"Don't count on it."

I stared down the highway. The aspen borders were starting to lose their color.

I imagined the evergreens heavy with snow. They seemed to march toward us, an unstoppable army.

* * *

"I want to move here," Stephen said as we passed the ENTERING MOTHERLODE sign. He'd been oohing and ahhing at natural wonders for the last 20 miles or so, hunting for the names of trees and rocks on his phone and, unfortunately, sharing them all with me.

"Look at those cliffs," he said. "And that waterfall. Did you see it?"

I grunted. "I'm driving."

"Am I supposed to feel lightheaded yet? I don't."

"Wait 'til we get out of the car."

He stared at the shops, the park, the miniature fire station. When we passed *Le Coeur D'Or,* he whistled. "Looks fancy. I want to eat there sometime."

"Not if I'm paying. It *is* dinner time, though. There's a little place down the road I think you'll like."

A couple of minutes later I pulled into the Ore Cart parking lot.

"Is everything here named after something having to do with mining?"

"Pretty much."

"I love that, don't you?"

"Can't get enough of it."

He unhooked his seatbelt. "So this is high altitude. Here goes nothin'." He climbed out carefully, then stood there. "I feel fine."

"Maybe it only affects women."

"You said it, not me."

He ordered the Gold Pan Panini, maybe for the alliteration. I had the Baby Blackjack Burger for financial reasons.

Afterward we proceeded to the Lodgepole Inn, still the only affordable place with a vacancy. I hadn't prepared him to meet the Cranky Old Woman, wanting it to be a surprise.

When we entered the office, I could hear a television set somewhere in the back. I buzzed the buzzer.

The ancient one took her time getting to the front desk. This time her sweater was a faded blue, matching the veins in the backs of her hands.

She scanned Stephen with narrowed eyes. "You're in Cabin Eight. You . . . planning to . . . stay there tonight?"

"Of course."

"I mean *stay* there."

"I'm not sure what you—"

"Just asking. I run a respectable place here."

He stifled a grin. "You can't be too careful."

The woman grunted, still looking suspicious. "Your cabin's same as hers. Except we haven't had any complaints about your toilet."

"Thank goodness."

After taking a key from the board on the wall, the woman set it on the counter. "No loud music."

"Right. I'll leave my electric guitar in the trunk."

We turned to go, but he stopped when he saw the rack of

brochures. He pulled out a copy of *Motherlode Monthly* and started leafing through it.

"Man, I want to see all these places," he said.

"Not tonight," I said.

"They light up the volcanic cliffs after dark. Have you seen that?"

"Somehow I missed it."

"There's an annual community theater historical production in the park. No, wait. They had that already."

"I'm sure it was stellar."

"There's an article about a mine. I've always wanted to go in a mine. My favorite part of *Sleeping Beauty* was when the dwarfs went off to work with their pickaxes."

"You want to go to the Victory Mine?"

"Yeah. But I can't find anything about tours."

"They don't have them anymore. That's where I met Troy Gant, remember?"

He tucked the magazine under his arm. "I can dream, can't I? Speaking of which, I think I'll retire to Cabin Eight. Been kind of a long day."

I led him there, hearing his suitcase trundle along on the gravel behind me.

"She's a riot, isn't she?" he asked.

"Who?"

"The woman at the front desk."

"We've had our moments."

"Seems to think there's something shady going on."

"That about sums up her worldview."

"'Night," he said, stepping into his cabin and hoisting his suitcase over the threshold.

"'Night."

I walked to Cabin Six, wondering how I'd pass the time until I could fall asleep. I turned the key in the lock.

I flipped on the light and shut the door behind me.

It took a few seconds to realize something was wrong.

The bedspread was rumpled on the floor. Three dresser drawers were open, as was the closet door.

But the most important things were those I didn't see.

My laptop was gone. The AC adapter was still there, but unattached.

I looked in the closet. The hatbox was missing.

I swallowed.

Marvin came to mind. I pictured him opening the door to his home office, only to be startled by a whack from behind. I rubbed the back of my neck.

Now I knew how I'd be passing the time this evening.

Whether I'd ever go to sleep, however, was something else.

CHAPTER 12

SHERIFF TANAKA LOOKED A LITTLE TOO EAGER WHEN HE showed up on my doorstep, responding to my 911 call no more than 15 minutes after I'd placed it.

The deputy behind him didn't. He was thirtyish, red-haired, freckled, frowning. I decided to think of him as Deputy Crabb.

The two men stepped inside. "Hear you've had some trouble, Ms. Neville," the sheriff said.

"Trouble, yeah." I was still off balance, finding it hard to focus. I waved in the general direction of the closet. "A break-in, I think."

"Yes, I can see that. Anything missing?"

"A laptop. And the hatbox I showed you earlier."

He shook his head. "That's not good."

Deputy Crabb pulled a notebook and pen from his pocket and started taking notes, his frown deepening.

The sheriff's gaze fell on Stephen, who was sitting on a chair in the corner. "And who's this?"

I introduced him. "He's just joined me to help with the research on our book," I added.

Tanaka nodded. "Looks like you're just in time." He turned to the deputy. "Lloyd, go get the manager, okay?"

Just as the deputy reached the door, it opened. The Cranky Old Woman stuck her head in.

"What's going on?" she demanded.

"Edna, your guest has had some things taken." He bent down and examined the lock. "No forced entry. Must have copied the key or stolen it." He paused. "Is there a key missing?"

"How should I know?"

"By looking, I imagine. Could you do that?"

She muttered something I couldn't hear, then left.

He turned toward me. "Anything else taken?"

"No."

"Pretty obvious the perpetrator was after information. Lloyd, you want to take a look around?"

Deputy Crabb put away his pad and pen. "Be right back," he said.

The sheriff looked at me, then Stephen. "When's the last time you were in here?"

"About five-thirty this morning," I said.

"I've *never* been in here," Stephen added.

"So maybe somebody saw this person. He or she had all day to do it."

The door opened again. It was Deputy Crabb, who held a roll of wide, yellow plastic tape. Looking around as if to find the perfect spot, he stretched a length of it between his hands. SHERIFF'S LINE DO NOT CROSS, it said.

"We don't need that," the sheriff said.

"But—"

"Just dust for prints."

The door opened again.

"Yeah, the key's gone," the old woman said.

"Who has access to the keys?"

She shrugged. "I don't know."

"Anybody who walks into the office when you're not at the desk can take one?"

She lifted her chin in defiance. "I can't be expected to stand there twenty-four hours a day. I have a life, too, you know."

"I'm sure you do, Edna. We're going to poke around here a little more. Feel free to go back to your business."

She was about to leave when she spotted Stephen. "How long have *you* been here?" she asked.

"Since Carolyn called and told me what happened."

"Are you leaving soon?"

Stephen rolled his eyes. "As soon as possible."

"Have to get the lock changed in the morning," she mumbled. "Locksmith is a thief himself. Hundred dollars for a house call, and that's before he fixes anything. You people are costing me money."

When she'd left, the sheriff turned to his deputy. "Find anything, Lloyd?"

"Not seeing any prints. Perpetrator must have worn gloves."

The sheriff shook his head. "I'll do what I can, Ms. Neville. But to be honest with you, only about ten percent of burglaries get solved. Not just here, but all over. And we don't have the manpower to give it a higher priority."

I frowned. "But this involves evidence in a murder."

"I know. At least the hatbox should be easier to identify than the laptop. If it hasn't been destroyed." He paused. "Let's go, Lloyd. We'll be in touch with you folks."

It was quiet after they'd gone.

Stephen stood up. "I hope you'll be all right."

"I'll be fine."

"'Night again."

"'Night."

When the door closed, I looked around. Until that lock was changed, the door might as well be wide open.

I got up and used the chair Stephen had been sitting on to brace the door shut, which of course would do no good against the holder of my key. I searched the cabin for anything I could use against an intruder. All I could find was a wooden-handled toilet plunger in the bathroom, the short kind. I tried to imagine how I'd use it, but smothering an intruder's face with the pink rubber cup seemed a pretty ineffective method of self-defense.

Stepping outside in the dark, I ventured to the rental car. In the trunk I found a foot-long tire iron. Not as hefty as the one I remembered from my father's Oldsmobile, but it seemed to have more potential than the plunger.

I set it on the nightstand. Finally I turned off the lights, except the one in the bathroom.

For the rest of the night I sat in bed, dozing off occasionally and waking myself up, listening for a faint latch click that never came.

* * *

In the morning all was as I'd left it.

I was almost glad to be alive.

Stephen and I had breakfast at the Ore Cart, talking mainly about the break-in. About halfway through his Grubstake Waffle, he rerouted our conversation.

"I'd like to meet this lady," he said.

"Who?"

"Rose. The one you talked about. When we're done eating, let's go to her shop. Is it open yet?"

"It will be."

A few minutes later I paid the check, then drove us there. The stool-dwelling teenager wasn't on duty. Rose was at the counter, back to wearing the pale pink business suit, using a giant black marking pen on a paper banner the size of a card table. The closer we got, the stronger the solvent fumes were. She'd gotten as far as writing INVENT when she looked up.

"Carolyn," she said, trying to wrinkle her nose and smile at the same time. "Sorry about the smell." She capped the marker.

"*Invent*?" I asked.

"Inventory Reduction Sale. It's that time of year, and I hate counting."

Her gaze traveled to Stephen. "Morning," she said.

"Rose, this is my senior editor, Stephen Ames. Stephen, Rose MacIlhenny."

"Nice to meet you," he said, shaking her hand. "Carolyn says you've been a big help in trying to put the book together."

She shrugged. "Well, I was fortunate to have Iris's letters. And now you do."

I cleared my throat. "Not anymore."

She turned to me. "What do you mean?"

"The hatbox was stolen last night."

She gasped. "No!"

"Along with my laptop. Somebody got a key to my cabin. Obviously he or she doesn't want us to know what happened to Iris."

"You could have been attacked, like your friend Marvin."

"That did occur to me."

"What are you going to do?"

"The sheriff's looking into it. But he's not optimistic about finding anything." I paused. "I'm sorry. I know those letters mean a lot to you."

"Not more than your safety," she said.

The door opened. Two women came in, looking around and whispering about the marker smell.

"Well, you have business to attend to," I said.

"Nice to meet you," Stephen repeated. "Just wanted to say hello."

Leaning over the counter, Rose looked me in the eye. "You keep me posted. And stay safe."

"I'll try."

She headed for her customers as we went outside.

We paused on the sidewalk. "Nice lady," Stephen said.

"Yes."

"I'm glad she's helping out." But there was something in his expression that didn't fit his words, as if he'd just had a disturbing thought but didn't want to share it.

"Time to move on, I guess," he said. "Let's go see whether that lock has been changed."

I set out for the car, wondering what was going on.

* * *

The Cranky Old Woman, whose name I now knew was Edna, was behind the front desk. She hugged the afghan to herself as if we might take it away.

"No, I don't have your key," she announced. "Locksmith isn't coming 'til this afternoon. And it's going to cost me two hundred bucks to get the lock changed. I hope you're proud of yourself."

I concocted a smile of sorts. "I was wondering," I said, "whether you saw or heard anything at all yesterday—a vehicle, a person—that might provide a clue about who got into my cabin."

"No. Just like I told the deputy. I can't be expected to know everything that happens twenty-four hours a day."

"Of course not." I paused. "Is there a reason why the keys aren't kept in a locked case?"

She slapped both hands on the counter and leaned

forward. "If you don't like the way I run the place, you're welcome to go elsewhere."

Folding my hands, I tried for the demeanor of an exceptionally patient kindergarten teacher. "I'll certainly take that under advisement. In the meantime, we'll be back later for the new key."

In the parking lot I turned to Stephen. "She seems open to our leaving," I said.

"She's nothing if not flexible."

I frowned. "In light of what happened last night, I'm beginning to wonder whether it's a good idea to stay in Motherlode at all."

He was silent for a moment. "Did I mention how Marvin and Tracy are doing these days? I'm sure they'd be happy to trade places with us."

I flinched.

"Sorry," he said. "That was a low blow."

"Say no more."

And he didn't.

He didn't have to.

CHAPTER 13

At lunchtime I introduced Stephen to the dazzling selection of prepackaged sandwiches at the convenience store, which today featured tuna salad and beef with cheddar, both of which required a checking of expiration dates due to their unusually yellowish bread. Two tables adorned the patio outside, still shaded by blue Bud Lite umbrellas despite the sun's apparent unwillingness to generate heat to match its light.

"It's too cold out here," I said as soon as I sat down.

"I'm not eating in the car when there's so much to see," he said. "Look at that cliff."

"It's a cliff, alright."

He munched for a few moments, then pulled a couple of brochures from his pocket. "Can we go somewhere this afternoon?"

"We have a job to do."

"But aren't we kind of on hold? We have to wait for the sheriff's office to get that handwriting analysis. And anything they might come up with from your cabin."

"What did you have in mind?"

"I want to see the cliffs light up."

I glanced at the sky. "Too early."

"I also want to go to a mine."

"I believe we covered that. The Victory Mine doesn't have tours anymore."

"I could at least see the outside of it. This might be my only chance."

I sipped my coffee, wishing it were 30 degrees hotter. "Assuming Troy Gant is there, he's pretty obnoxious. I don't think you'd like him."

He shrugged. "I'm used to handling obnoxious people."

"Are we talking about anyone in particular?"

"Not *just* you."

"All right, we'll go. But don't say I didn't warn you."

* * *

Fall colors were nowhere to be found as we rode to the Victory Mine, but Stephen's enthusiasm was undampened. By the time we reached the gate, his memories of the Seven Dwarfs' diamond mine and the words to "Heigh-Ho" had been thoroughly and needlessly refreshed.

We passed the shiny black SUV on our way into the little brick office. The door was open.

"Hey!" Gant cried when he saw me, as if he'd thought of no one else since our first meeting. He may not have been disrobing me with his eyes, but he was at least removing my coat.

Stephen seemed not to notice. I stepped forward and introduced him.

"Senior Editor, eh?" Gant said with a grin. "Sounds way too old for such a young guy."

Stephen smiled. "I'll bet you say that to all the tourists."

Leaning back in his chair, he shook his head. "Unfortunately, we don't get tourists anymore. Or maybe I should say *yet*."

"Well, you have two now," he said. "I've wanted to see a mine since I was a little kid."

I shrugged. "I tried to tell him you don't do tours anymore, Mr. Gant."

He held up a small spiral notebook. "As a matter of fact, I was just working on that. This is my tour guide script. Most of it. Took the one they used back in the seventies and brought it up to date."

"Just in case you ever start tours again?" I asked.

"Oh, we'll have tours, Ms. Neville. I just spent a small fortune having the elevator updated. If you'd like, I can take you down there. It'll give me a chance to practice my spiel."

Stephen grinned. "You mean we can see the mine? Now?"

"That's exactly what I mean."

I hesitated. "Descend into the bowels of the earth?"

He chuckled. "That's one way to put it. A full nine hundred and seventy feet. Perfectly safe. Tested it myself two days ago."

"Oh, come on, Carolyn," Stephen said. "This is the opportunity of a lifetime."

I threw up my hands in surrender. "Where do we start?"

Standing up, Gant stuffed the spiral notebook in the back pocket of his designer jeans. "Right here. You'll need a helmet." He went to the empty desk in the corner, where a large cardboard box sat next to the chair. "Pick your color."

They were metal helmets, scuffed and dented but intact, more rounded than the ones construction workers wear. He extracted a yellow one. Stephen chose dark green. Mine was white, or had been a decade or two ago.

Gant pulled on a light jacket. "Gonna be a little chilly down there. Follow me."

There was a trail behind the building, sloping down about

a hundred feet to a heap of what looked like gravel. A narrow-gauge track, bent and missing about half its ties, sat atop the mound, leading into a dilapidated wooden structure on stilts.

I stared. "You can't be serious. That isn't—"

He laughed. "No, it's not. That's the old mine entrance. Almost a hundred years old. Keep going."

The trail took us through a stand of evergreens, then to a view that brought us all to a halt. Another hundred feet away stood a gray steel tower with a pulley at the top, half-circled by wooden poles lofting power lines and transformers.

Stephen beamed. An excited squeak leaked out.

"There she is," Gant said. "I'm hoping we can put in a tram to get people down this hill. Or at least a paved ramp for wheelchairs. Otherwise the ADA lawyers will have a field day."

We made it to the entrance without those amenities. But it was not the sort of entrance you see in historical photos, with timbers and lanterns. It was just a large steel door with an AUTHORIZED PERSONNEL ONLY sign.

He got out a ring of keys and unlocked it. The smells of stale air and machine oil drifted out.

The elevator looked like a cage, heavy red steel, big enough to carry half a dozen people comfortably—or ten people much less so. Rust pocked the paint.

Gant pulled out his spiral notebook. "Okay, this is where my spiel kicks in." He cleared his throat. "Afternoon, folks. Welcome to the Victory Mine. Are you ready to take a journey nine hundred and seventy-five feet closer to the center of the earth?"

"Yeah!" Stephen said.

"If necessary," I muttered.

"This is what we call the cage," he said, which didn't sound very imaginative. "Step right in, and please move to the back of the car." We did so. He joined us, then pulled the door shut behind him and pressed a red button on the wall. There was a buzzing sound, then a feeling that my stomach was migrating upward between my shoulders.

We were going down, fast. I looked around for something to hold onto. No handles presented themselves; a few narrow bars of metal were welded to the walls, barely enough to grasp with two fingers, which I did with a vengeance. I could see where tourists over the years had scratched their initials into the paint but had no desire to follow suit.

The cage swayed slightly. Every so often there was a banging sound. My ears popped.

"I love it!" Stephen cried.

"In a moment you'll see a red light go by," Gant said. "That means we're halfway there."

Sure enough, the light shot past. So did a yellow light, and the sight of tunnels running off into blackness. More lights, more tunnels, more ear-popping. I tried to remember whether I'd updated my will.

Eventually the cage slowed, then barely crept, then stopped. There was a rhythmic *clack clack*, then a clanking noise.

We exited, my legs briefly threatening to betray me, and found ourselves facing a sign:

YOU ARE NOW 975 FEET UNDERGROUND!

The air was cold, clammy. I folded my arms, counting on my tweedy brown blazer for warmth. Stephen hugged himself, his thin, black sweater probably inadequate.

I looked ahead in the tunnel. It was higher than most residential ceilings, blasted through rough granite that was mostly pink or gray depending on the light. Some kind of white crystals coated the rock like mold.

"Gross," Stephen said. "What's the white stuff?"

Gant consulted his notes. "Epsom salts. It leaches from the rock." He flipped the pages backward. "Folks, please move back so that everyone can hear me. Thank you." He paused as if we were a much bigger group, then continued. "Gold was first discovered in this region in 1886 by a prospector named Edgar Auchincloss. He staked his claim quickly, calling it the Victory Mine. The town of Motherlode was established two years later, and its population ballooned from two-fifty to twelve thousand in a single year. The town was notorious for its saloons, gambling, and brothels as well as its corrupt politicians. Worst of all was . . ."

I tuned out, wondering whether eminent historian Arthur Keebler knew his speech had been plagiarized. Or maybe it was on purpose, and Gant planned to sell Keebler's book in the gift shop. Either way, he was losing me.

As my mind wandered, so did my gaze. Down a side shaft I noticed old wooden ladders and heavy beams. I imagined the ghosts of miners past climbing up and down like angels on Jacob's Ladder, doing whatever miners did besides going on strike, getting buried alive in cave-ins, and being memorialized in depressing poetry and songs.

Next thing I knew, Gant and Stephen were leaving me behind, walking further into the tunnel over the old rails. I caught up, squinting at the oversized round bulbs that hung every 10 feet or so from a single wire over my head.

Along the path were nooks containing rusty, riveted drums the size of meat smokers at a county fair. Gant didn't explain their nature or purpose, which suited me just fine, given my lack of curiosity.

Suddenly he stopped in a wide spot. Some kind of mechanism was propped against the wall, a tangle of red rubber hose, green and gray pipe, brass fittings, and a long, coppery tube. A dusty red wooden crate with EXPLOSIVES stenciled on the side sat like a stage prop next to it.

"Who knows how the miners got the ore out of the rock?" Gant asked.

"Dynamite!" Stephen said.

"Nope. That was mainly for excavating tunnels."

Stephen made a disgusted noise. "Not fair. It's misleading to have a box of it right there when you ask the question."

Gant glanced down at his pad. "I'll make a note of that," he said, but didn't.

"Okay, then, with a drill," Stephen added.

"That's right, young man." He picked up the apparatus as if it were a machine gun and pointed it at the wall. "I'd advise you folks to cover your ears. Miners have the worst hearing loss of any occupation in America."

Clapping our hands over our ears, we braced ourselves. He squeezed the trigger. There was a hiss, then a rapid banging. It lasted only a few moments, followed by another hiss, then silence. He put the drill back down.

"You didn't use earplugs," I said.

"It was only a couple seconds," he said.

"But it sets a bad example, don't you think?"

"I'll make a note of that, too." He paused to not do so, then continued. "Now, look around. Do you see any gold nuggets?"

I couldn't help looking, though the answer was obvious.

"No," Stephen said.

"Chances are you won't. What you should look for is a vein. They're tiny." He pointed at the wall, to a spot with a purple stripe. "That's fluorite. It's a hint there might be gold in them thar hills."

His attempt at bucolic inflection fell short, but we let it pass.

He rattled off a description of what happens after a vein is discovered, something about mercury and cyanide and burning off the rock and pouring the gold into bars and buttons. I was looking around at the high metal ladders and the turquoise-colored drips that hung like candle wax from the ceiling here and there, crystallized.

"Any questions?" he said.

Stephen raised his hand. "Did any miners ever die here?"

"Unfortunately, yes. In the many years the mine was operational, a total of 74 men were lost. But our safety record was one of the best in the state of Colorado." He sounded a little defensive. "Any other questions?"

There being none, he circled around us. "Then it's time to go back the way we came."

We trudged in that direction. Stephen kept peering at the walls. "Looking for a vein," he said.

"Why?" I asked. "If you find gold, you don't get to keep it."

He shook his head. "You just don't get it."

"Apparently not."

He snapped about a dozen photos with his phone on the way back, including one of me. I managed to smile.

Eventually we were back at the cage. "So, what did you think?" Gant asked.

"Fascinating," I said, wanting to get back to the surface as quickly as possible.

Stephen looked thoughtful. "Maybe it needs more . . . I don't know, a little more audience participation."

"Like what?"

"You could turn out the lights and pretend you're all trapped."

He shook his head. "Insurance issues. Heart attacks, stuff like that."

"Oh. Never mind."

"I was thinking about putting in a pneumatic-driven train, though. Looks like a ride at Disneyland, rollercoaster-type cars all different colors. Sounds like a riding lawn-mower, but quieter and no fumes. All we need is enough investors. Which we'll get, definitely. No question."

There was an awkward pause. "Okay," Gant said. "Time to go back up. Watch your heads."

We all got in the cage. He yanked the door shut, then pushed the red button.

This time there was no buzzing sound.

He pressed the button again.

Then once more.

I swallowed.

"Well," he said.

"What's going on?" Stephen asked, his eyes wide.

Gant looked up at the lights. "We've got power. It's not that."

"Has this . . . happened before?" I asked.

"Not to me."

I pulled my phone from my purse and tapped the screen. NO SERVICE, it said.

Vowing not to panic, I looked around. There was the sign on the wall.

YOU ARE NOW 975 FEET UNDERGROUND!

I broke my vow immediately. *Help, God,* I thought.

"Not to worry, folks," Gant said. "This elevator has a dedicated landline to the volunteer fire department in town."

"Sounds good," Stephen said, sinking back against the cage.

Gant unlocked a door next to the button and picked up a red receiver. "We have a dial tone."

"Yes!" Stephen said.

Gant listened. Finally he straightened up, alert. "Yeah, this is Troy Gant at the Victory Mine. Calling from the elevator in the shaft. We're stuck at the bottom."

There was a pause. "Well, you guys are supposed to come out and reset it at the top."

Another pause. "The manual tells you how."

Still another pause. "Well, *I* don't know where you put the manual. Is anybody else there?"

He listened. "He's at the market? When do you expect him back?"

One more pause. Gant covered his eyes with his hand. "Just get here as soon as you can."

He hung up. I felt like whimpering, but Stephen did it for me.

Gant swore. "I don't know why they call them first responders."

We stared at each other, then down at the cage floor, then around at the tunnel walls. The weight of 975 feet of rock seemed to be pressing the air from my lungs.

I could see where this was going. Eventually we'd go insane, if not from claustrophobia, then from sheer boredom.

"I suggest we wait outside the elevator," I said.

"Fine," Gant said.

There were no chairs, only three more inauthentic EXPLOSIVES crates and a small barrel that said GUNPOWDER on the side. We settled down on the former, facing each other.

"What happens if the reset button doesn't work?" Stephen asked.

Gant leaned forward, elbows on knees. "We'd have to call the elevator company. They probably have a repairman in Copper Ridge. Maybe."

"So we could be here for days," I said.

He smiled. "I doubt that."

"Is there any water?" Stephen asked.

Gant scratched his chin. "Yeah, although the pipes may be rusty."

"Any food?"

He turned to me. "Not unless you have some in your purse."

I opened it and poked around. "Cough drops." My stomach growled.

Stephen looked up at the ceiling. "What if we have to . . ."

"Use the bathroom?" Gant asked. "There's a toilet. The feds require at least one."

We all sat there, having exhausted the most obvious topics of conversation. But Gant managed to find another.

"So, Ms. Neville," he said, turning in my direction. "You know plenty about me, but I know zip about you."

"I'm not very interesting," I said.

"I doubt that. You do . . . editing stuff, right?"

"Yep."

"You like it?"

"Sometimes."

"Pardon me for noticing, but I see there's no wedding band on your finger. I take it you're single."

I frowned. "Judging from the other ring fingers down here, I take it we're *all* single."

"What's it like to date in New York? Is it all nightclubs, or what?"

"Only if you want it to be."

He grinned. "I imagine you don't want it to be. But I'll bet the guys wish you did."

"Well, New York probably isn't that much different from Denver. People are the same wherever you go. Unbearable."

"Hey, all I know is you'd be very popular here. With good reason."

Stephen got up, looking ready to whup somebody's butt.

I held up a cautionary hand, then took out my notepad and pen. "You know, Mr. Gant, this might be a good chance for you to tell us more about your parents. For the book."

"Oh." He gave me a skeptical look. "What's left to talk about?"

"I saw in *Darkness at Dawn* that your father liked hunting."

He nodded. "Never forget the time he took me to look for elk. I was about twelve. We were in the woods pretty much all day. Finally he got a bead on a good-sized bull. He was about to pull the trigger when I looked down at the ground and thought I saw a rattlesnake. I let out a screech, and he missed his shot."

He shook his head. "Man, did he give me hell about that. Said there were no rattlers in Motherlode, and he was right. The snake was a stick."

I paused in my note-taking. "And he liked target shooting."

"Had targets set up about a hundred yards from the mine. I kind of liked it, going out there with my little twenty-two and trying to hit that bullseye. Wasn't very good at it, though. He always gave me a hard time. Said I shot like a girl."

I shook my head. "So your father was fond of guns," I said. I'd known plenty of people who were, back in Idaho. They'd seemed normal enough.

He leaned forward on his elbows again. "Ms. Neville, if you're trying to make a connection between being a sportsman and strangling people, good luck."

"No, I'm just—"

"I know people like you see guns in a whole other way. My dad had high standards, but he wasn't violent. Unless you count spanking, which I suppose you do."

"She doesn't," Stephen chimed in. "But *I* do."

Gant folded his arms across his chest. "Dad had his faults. But he gave back to the community. Kept the mine open. Loved dressing up in those old-time suits for the annual Founder's Day parade, that sort of thing."

I could see we'd reached the limit on that subject for the time being. I turned to the next page of my pad. "How about your mother?"

He shrugged. "What can I say? Kids love their mothers. I loved mine."

"What did you love most about her?"

He patted the sides of his EXPLOSIVE crate. "When my father and I had a . . . difference of opinion, she always took my side. More than I deserved, probably."

"Your mom and dad had . . . a good relationship?"

"Sure. She liked nice things, especially clothes. He was always buying her things. Bought her a camel once, just because she'd seen one in *National Geographic* and thought they were cool or something."

"But did they have a truly—"

"Look," he said. "I know all about your friend's theory that my father was after Iris. It's a lie. He gave Mom everything she ever wanted."

End of story, I thought. If our fate was to spend a lot of time trapped 975 feet below the earth's surface, we didn't need to be at each other's throats.

Stowing my pad in my purse, I searched our surroundings for a new topic. Almost instantly one presented itself. I felt the need to use that federally mandated toilet.

"Uh . . . where's the restroom you mentioned?"

He pointed down the tunnel. "Next shaft on the right. Can't guarantee there's any paper, though. Been a while since I checked."

When I got there, I was surprised to see the place had an actual door with the customary icon. Flipping on the light switch, I beheld what looked like a giant black ice chest dotted with rivets. Twin seats, the lids of which were both up, had a vertical valve wheel situated between them. There was even a roll of paper.

All went as expected, with the minor complication of near-arctic temperature. The sink water ran brown as cider, but the paper towels were first-rate.

When I returned, Gant and Stephen seemed not to have found a topic of conversation. I didn't share my restroom review, nor did they inquire.

I consulted my watch. It was so quiet I could actually hear the ticking.

All at once a sharp ringing splintered the silence. We all jumped.

It was the red phone.

Gant ran to pick it up. "Hello?"

He listened. "Where are you? The office? You can't reset from there. Go to the mine entrance. Down the hill."

He hung up. "They'll call back."

Five minutes later the phone jangled again. "Did you find the button? Look at the gate at the top of the elevator shaft. To the right." He paused. "A red button with white letters saying RESET."

More waiting. Finally he said, "Now push it."

I held my breath.

"I—I don't hear anything," Stephen said.

"Nothing to hear," Gant said. "We have to push *our* button. Time to get in the cage."

We did, and Gant pulled the door shut with a *clang*. He

stabbed the button with his thumb. There was a loud buzz, a groan of metal, and slowly the floor seemed to fall away.

Stephen actually clapped.

Our ascent took longer than our descent. Rocking back and forth, we watched the lights and slowed to a crawl at last. When we halted there was a *clack clack*, then a final *clank*.

The air felt warm again. Gant pushed the door open.

Two middle-aged firefighters stood there, looking proud of themselves. Their uniforms looked too clean to have gotten within shouting distance of an actual blaze.

"Hey, Mr. Gant," said the taller one. "We did it!"

"Yeah, you did it," he muttered.

"You guys all right?" asked the shorter one.

Stephen nodded. I replied by staggering out of the cage and onto solid ground.

"Boy," said the taller one. "We're gonna have to tell the newspapers about this. It's like those miners in Chile."

Gant stepped forward, his index finger in the fireman's face. "You will *not* tell the papers about this. Or anybody else."

"Why not?"

"If this gets out, nobody's ever going to come here. They'll think the elevator's gonna kill them."

The firefighters glanced at each other. "Okay," said the taller one. They turned and trudged back toward the office, their rubber boots looking out of place in the dust.

"Thank you!" Stephen called. They waved without looking back.

"Well, you wanted an adventure," Gant said, locking the door behind us.

"It was incredible," Stephen said.

Gant turned to me. "And what did you think, Ms. Neville?"

"Worth every penny," I said, and did my own trudging in the firemen's footsteps.

* * *

I was still failing to tingle with enthusiasm when we sat at the Ore Cart that evening, dining on dishes whose clever names I could no longer bear to say aloud. Stephen insisted on reliving our experience, his eyes glistening and his hands stirring the air with such vigor that other patrons must have thought I was deaf.

"Maybe you should immortalize this in a bleak and maudlin poem," I said.

"Do you want to see the pictures again?"

I shook my head. "I don't want to look at the lit-up cliffs tonight, either. I've had my fill of sightseeing."

He shrugged. "I guess we've done enough for—"

The *1812 Overture* beckoned from my pocket. I hauled out my phone, so tired that it seemed heavier than usual.

Tracy was calling.

"Carolyn?"

"Yes, how are you? I haven't been able to—"

"Carolyn, I've been trying to get hold of you all day."

"We've been . . . tied up."

"You won't believe what's happened."

I was afraid to say anything.

"Marvin. He's awake, praise God!"

I paused. "You're serious."

"Of course. Now, when I say *awake*, I mean sort of."

I looked at Stephen, wanting to put the call on speaker, but not here.

"How is he *sort* of awake?" I asked.

Stephen's eyebrows went up.

"It happened about nine-thirty this morning. I dozed off

after the doctor made his rounds, and all of a sudden I heard this voice saying my name. Didn't sound like Marvin. Too phlegmy or something. But it was him."

"Wow."

"At first all he could say was my name. But as the day went on, he got so he knows who he is and who I am. And he can feed himself."

"I don't know what to say. Do they know whether he's going to stay awake?"

"He's asleep right now. But it's normal sleep. And no, they aren't sure. But they say it's a positive sign."

"That's great."

She yawned. "It's pretty late here. For me, anyway. Keep praying."

"I will. Maybe I can get Stephen to try it."

"You do that. Goodnight."

I put the phone down.

Stephen looked at me. "Something's changed."

"Yeah," I said. "Everything."

CHAPTER 14

We were on our way to breakfast the next morning when Tracy called back. My heart rate shot up as I pulled over in front of the thrift shop.

"Carolyn? I'm handing the phone to Marvin."

I bit my lip. For a while I heard only the beep of a monitor.

Finally a voice, hoarse from disuse, came on the line. "Hello?"

"Marvin, it's Carolyn."

"Hello," he said again. I waited to hear *Cranberry*, but it didn't come.

Stephen leaned closer. "Marvin, this is Stephen. I'm here, too."

"Good," he said. There was a lengthy pause. "I'm in the hospital," he continued. "The rehab center, they call it."

"I know," I said. "We're sorry."

"They tell me I got hit in the head." Another pause. "I just ate breakfast. Eggs and toast. Have you eaten yet?"

"I will soon."

"Where are you?"

"In Colorado. A town called Motherlode."

"What are you doing there?"

I looked at Stephen, who looked at me. We both sighed.

"We're working on a project you started," I said. "A book."

Another long pause.

"*Darkness at Dawn*," he said finally.

I couldn't help smiling. Apparently authors never forgot their bestsellers.

"Marvin, do you know who hit you?" I asked.

"No," he said. "It was too dark."

"Do you recall visiting Motherlode and talking to George Svoboda about who killed Iris MacIlhenny?"

Another pause.

"Who?"

I closed my eyes.

There was a rustling on the line. Tracy was back. "The nurse wants Marvin to rest now. I'll try calling tomorrow."

"Please do," I said.

With a groan I put down the phone. "Everything's changed, all right."

Stephen looked out his window. "Maybe he's not up to speed yet, but he's alive."

I shook my head.

"I'm not sure Marvin would call that living," I said.

* * *

Breakfast was eaten largely in silence. From there we returned to the Lodgepole Inn, where we debated our next move.

We settled on wandering around the parking lot. But not aimlessly.

"Look for clues as to who might have stolen my key and broken into my cabin," I said.

"Such as?"

"Tire tracks. An earring. I don't know."

It was just cold enough to make the job unpleasant. Tires left little behind on gravel, and dead leaves obscured the rest. To no one's surprise, we found nothing. Or maybe we did and didn't realize it.

"You know, I've been thinking," Stephen said. "Whoever hit Marvin, and presumably broke into your cabin, couldn't have been in Motherlode when Marvin was attacked, right?"

I thought for a moment. "That person was in Florida."

"So we need to find out which suspects weren't here then. Get their alibis."

"Well, we can't ask Skye," I said. "Even if he's alive. That leaves Gant."

He cleared his throat. "And . . . Rose."

I gaped at him. *"Rose?"*

"I know you don't want to consider that possibility, but—"

"Rose? Can you imagine her strangling her sister? Hitting an old man from behind with a lead pipe?"

"No. But it's not impossible."

So that was why he'd looked so weird after meeting Rose.

I shook my head. "I can't ask her where she was when Marvin was hit. How would *you* feel if I asked you that question?"

"Angry, of course. But I'd know you were just doing your job. Especially if you complimented her first. Softens the blow."

"Thanks. I think I know a little more about social interaction than certain other people in this parking lot."

He shrugged.

I looked around the lot one more time, hoping for rescue. None appeared.

"Let's try Gant first," I said.

"Great. You can practice on him."

Frowning, I headed for the car.

* * *

Returning to the Victory Mine was like revisiting a crosswalk where you'd been struck by a drunken driver and left for dead. Or having to read a Barbara Cartland novel.

Gant's black SUV was gone. So was Gant.

But someone was there, somebody who drove an old silver Subaru.

The office door was open. Gant's desk was unoccupied, but the opposite was true of the one in the corner. There sat a young woman, back to us, her hair bleached to the consistency of crabgrass in August, her attention held by her computer screen.

"Excuse me," I said.

Startled, she spun around. "Oh, hi! People! I can't believe it!"

"Can't believe what?"

"That you're people. I mean, I've never seen anybody here except Troy. Well, I saw the night security guy a couple times. But anyway . . ."

"We were looking for Mr. Gant, but maybe you can help us."

"I'm his secretary. Part-time."

We introduced ourselves.

"Bryton Palumbo," she said, extending her hand. She was an impressively shaped woman, a characteristic that didn't seem to escape Stephen's notice.

"How long have you worked for Mr. Gant?" I asked.

"About six months. Before that I handed out maps in Patriots' Park at the Motherlode Convention and Visitor Center. And played Dance Hall Girl Number Three at the community theater history play. Did you see it?"

"I wanted to," Stephen said. "We were too late."

"Troy's in Denver, arguing with some bureaucrat. Meanwhile I'm filling out forms for the EPA. I have to look up every third word online to figure out what it means."

For some reason that didn't surprise me. "Did Mr. Gant tell you about what happened with the elevator yesterday?"

Her eyebrows popped up. "No. Last time I saw him was three days ago."

We summarized. When we were done, she laughed.

"That's so *Troy*," she squealed.

"The reason we're here," I said, "is to find out something about his schedule. This was a couple of months ago."

She rolled her chair over to a wall calendar that had a picture of a terminally cute puppy on it. "Shoot," she said.

I asked where her boss was the week Marvin was attacked.

She frowned at the numbered squares. "I don't know. Wasn't around myself for most of that week. Boyfriend and I went to a casino in Central City."

"Oh," I said, disappointed.

"We didn't lose too much money. But afterward, we broke up."

"I'm sorry."

"No great loss. Anyway, Troy should be back tomorrow. You can ask him then."

We got up to leave. "Thank you," I said. We left the poor girl puzzling over the form on her desk. Maybe I needed to write a letter to the editor of *The Wall Street Journal* about the sorry state of education in this country.

When we sat in the car again, I turned to Stephen. "Where to?"

"You know where. You just don't want to go."

I turned the key in the ignition.

Unfortunately, it started.

* * *

Somehow I managed to convince Stephen we should have an early lunch at a bar and grill near the sheriff's office. He said I was stalling. He was right.

Every bite, mediocre as it was, seemed precious. Now I knew how condemned prisoners felt at their last meals. I resisted the urge to numb the apprehension with a shot of whiskey.

Afterward, things were busier than usual at Simply Rose, probably due to the Inventory Reduction Sale. Dax, the young man on the stool behind the counter, had found it necessary to abandon his perch and actually wait on customers. So did Rose, of course.

Stephen stood at my side, watching me watch the lady in pink. Eventually she untangled herself from her patrons and threaded the aisles toward us.

"Your sign must have worked," I said.

Rose put her hand over her heart. "Whew! Are you here to give me a break?"

I needed a compliment to soften the blow. One came to me, or I thought it did.

"You remind me of Margaret Thatcher," I said.

She blinked several times, as if I'd abruptly and awkwardly changed the subject. Which I had. "Pardon?"

"Margaret Thatcher. Former British Prime Minister."

She tilted her head to one side. "The Iron Lady?"

"Yes."

"Is it my hair? Or my lack of compassion?"

"Neither. You just . . . have what it takes."

Stephen looked at me as if I were about to crash my car into a concrete abutment.

"Can't say I'm a fan of Mrs. Thatcher," Rose said. "But I'm sure you meant it in a good way."

"The best," I said.

I tried my hand at a little throat-clearing, but there was no way to put it off any longer. "Rose, do you remember where you were the week Marvin was attacked?" I gave her the dates.

Her brow furrowed. "That's months ago." She headed for the register, and we followed. After pulling a Day-Timer from under the counter, she flipped the weeks backward and ran her fingernail across a page.

"Okay. I was out for three days."

"Why?" I asked.

She lowered her voice. "If you have to know, I was at home. Hung over, but mostly exhausted. It was the height of the season, and I was doing a little self-medicating. Dax covered for me."

"Did he actually see you during those three days?"

"Well, not exactly. I only talked to him on the phone."

I nodded. "So you can't—"

"Carolyn, what's this all about?"

I swallowed. "You . . . also remind me of Golda Meir."

"What?"

Stephen averted his eyes.

"Never mind," I said. "We . . . have to ask each suspect about his or her alibi."

She took a step back. "*Suspect? Alibi?*"

"Not that I think—"

"After I brought you those letters? After you and I talked about some very personal things?"

She looked around. Dax was being hailed by three customers at once.

"I have to get back to work," she said, and walked away.

I tried to sink into the floor.

But it turned out to be as solid as it looked.

CHAPTER 15

NEITHER OF US KNEW WHAT TO SAY AS I DROVE US BACK TO THE Lodgepole Inn.

I couldn't blame Rose. This whole thing had been cursed from the beginning, like a hotel built over an Indian burial ground.

When I stopped by the office to get my new key, the Cranky Old Woman almost threw it at me. I walked to my cabin; Stephen walked to his.

Sitting on my bed, I put in a call to the sheriff's office. Maybe they'd found some evidence in this cabin or heard from the handwriting expert.

"Sheriff's office, Deputy Ironhorse speaking."

So *that* was Deputy Ponytail's name. Far be it from me to insult a Native American, but I'd stick with the nickname. It worked with Deputy Crabb and the Cranky Old Woman. I was glad he couldn't read my thought about the Indian burial ground.

"This is Carolyn Neville. Is the sheriff around?"

"Nope. Sorry."

"Any news on the MacIlhenny case? A fingerprint, or something from the graphologist?"

"Nothing yet, Ms. Neville." He chuckled. "This isn't exactly the NYPD. We're lucky to have a fingerprint kit, much less a finger to use it on. And the handwriting expert only does this part-time."

"Right. Sorry to bother you."

I hung up. I was about to drown my sorrows in a glass of water when I heard a knock at the door.

"Housekeeping," said a male voice.

My jaw tensed. It didn't sound right. Too late in the day for maid service. I had the new key, but the burglar didn't. This time he'd need help to get in.

I went to the door and squinted through the peephole. There stood a shaggy-haired young man with a maintenance cart, halfway through a Snickers bar.

Repulsive? Yes.

Dangerous? Probably not.

I let him in. He looked about college age, though clearly not college material. As he wheeled a vacuum cleaner past me, I recognized a scent from my own alma mater. I'd never used pot myself, but most of the residents of my dorm had. *Sickly-sweet* was a cliché, but it wasn't far off the mark.

"Sorry I didn't do this already, ma'am. Kind of slept in late."

He looked around as if he'd forgotten why he'd entered, then switched the machine on and began to make slow passes on the carpet. I looked in my suitcase for earplugs but came up empty.

When he finally shut the thing down, my ears were ringing.

He carried in an armful of towels. As he did, something occurred to me.

"Were you here yesterday morning?" I asked.

There was a long pause as he looked at the floor.

"I . . . think so," he said.

"Did you see anything unusual? Maybe someone trying to get in?"

"No," he said slowly. "Was I supposed to?"

"No."

He went into the bathroom. "Although there was that one guy," he called.

"What guy?"

He came out, still carrying the towels. "Seemed to be in a big hurry to get out of the office and drive away." He paused. "At least I think it was a guy."

"What kind of vehicle was he driving?"

He frowned, thinking hard. "Not sure. Kind of big, I guess. Maybe a truck."

"What color?"

He tried again, but the neurons weren't firing. "No idea. Sorry."

He plodded through the rest of his routine, finishing by spritzing the air with something that smelled like vinegar. I handed him a dollar. I couldn't afford to pay him by the hour.

After he was gone, I sank back on the bed.

A probable guy in a possible truck.

It was true what they said.

A mind *was* a terrible thing to waste.

* * *

Around 5:00 p.m. I knocked on Stephen's door. He had the brochures spread out on the bed and sat down next to them.

When I told him about the housekeeping kid, he shook his head. "Now there's a clue you can use."

"Where do you want to get dinner?"

He picked up *Motherlode Monthly*. "There's a place called

Fresh Air. They have healthy dishes, like kale and kombucha. Can you believe it?"

"Sadly, I can."

"Let's not go there."

My phone interrupted. When I saw it was Tracy's number, I put it on speaker.

"You interested in an update?" she asked, and didn't wait for an answer. "Marvin's been up walking the halls today. And flirting with the nurse." She sounded almost irritated. "He's sitting in a chair by the bed now."

She put him on the line. "Hey, Cranberry," he said.

I smiled, my eyes welling up. His voice wasn't robust yet, but it wasn't feeble.

"You messing up all the groundwork I laid for this book?" he asked.

"We're doing our best."

"Don't give me that *we* stuff. You know you're the only one I've got doubts about."

"Marvin, do you recall talking to an old man named George Svoboda about who killed Iris MacIlhenny?"

"I do. Guy who saws up rocks in his backyard."

"Remember the sheriff?"

"Oh, yeah."

"And Art Keebler?"

He paused. "The history guy?"

"Right. Do you remember what you learned from them? Something you told us you couldn't go into yet?"

The lull was longer. Finally he said, "It's not there, girl. If I had my notes, maybe they'd jog my memory."

"The notes are gone. I looked. But don't worry. You'll get your thoughts together eventually."

"Hey," he said suddenly. "They're bringing dinner. Something brown on noodles. Not sure I want to find out what it is."

"At least you can eat it sitting in a chair. I'll let you go."

"Later."

I stuck the phone in my pocket.

"Sounds like he's doing pretty well," Stephen said.

"Better than that stoned housekeeper."

He checked his watch. "Speaking of dinner, I guess we're stuck with the Ore Cart."

That's where we went, and talked mostly about Marvin.

About halfway through the meal Stephen slipped a brochure from his pocket and waved it like a bidding card at an art auction. "Let's go to the cliffs tonight. With the lights."

"But it's going to be cold," I protested.

"All the more reason to go now. In a few days it'll be even colder."

We drove to the other side of town until we could see the cliffs, jutting like arrowheads from the ground. Sunset was in progress—not the most impressive I'd ever seen, but passably pink and periwinkle. After parking in a lot behind what looked like a soccer field, we waited. It took about 10 minutes for the horizon to be swallowed up in darkness.

Then the lights came on, shellacking the stone with red, green, yellow, blue. Climbing out of the car, we stared. We were the only ones in the lot.

"Oh, this was worth it," Stephen said. He tried to take a picture with his phone, but the image was too dim and grainy.

I shivered. Sure, the spectacle was impressive—in a gilding-the-lily sort of way. It was also freezing.

Stephen shivered, too.

I turned toward him. "Did you notice Gant's secretary today? Miss Palumbo?"

He looked like a deer in the headlights. "What do you mean?'

"Hey, it's okay. Sounds like she's available."

"I . . . but we're just here for a few—"

"I'm sure a relational expert like yourself doesn't need much time. Did I ever tell you about my first boyfriend?"

"I don't think so."

"Alden Barlow. We were in high school, junior year. He was editor of the literary magazine. The only guy in our school who had a beard. Almost nobody was interested in the magazine, so we had it pretty much to ourselves. But there was this other girl named Kathy who had a crush on Alden and kept telling him what a great writer he was, like Jack Kerouac. One day she told me he was going out with somebody else behind my back. I believed her, and made a big scene in the hallway. He broke up with me. A week later I found out she'd made it up, but I couldn't undo it."

"Is that meant to be encouraging?" he asked.

"Sure. I messed up that relationship, but it wasn't meant to be. If you and Miss Palumbo are meant to get together, you will."

He was too polite to mention that when it came to romance, I'd left behind a string of failures.

For a few more moments we stared at the regal outcroppings of rock that glowed against the dark sky.

He shivered again. So did I.

CHAPTER 16

AFTER BREAKFAST THE NEXT MORNING, I WONDERED WHETHER Troy Gant was at the mine yet. According to his secretary, he was supposed to be back today. What about that alibi?

My watch said he might be in, but I didn't want to drive all the way to his office again. So I went outside and tapped in his number.

"Victory Mine, Troy Gant speaking."

"Carolyn Neville. Good morning."

"I wish," he mumbled.

"I take it things didn't go well in Denver."

"Those people can't see past the ends of their noses. No vision. No imagination. How did Disney do it in Florida and California? Payoffs?"

"I don't know."

"I'm not giving up. But by the time we get every T crossed, I'll be too old to do the mine tour without a wheelchair." He paused. "Something I can do for you?"

"Stephen and I came by yesterday and talked with your secretary. Charming young woman."

"Must be why I hired her. God knows she can't spell."

"We were trying to confirm where you were the week Marvin Ainsley Pitts was attacked."

There was silence. "Why would you want to know that?"

I tried to think of a delicate way to phrase it. "To confirm that you weren't in Florida."

"Of course I wasn't in Florida. I've never been to Florida, except the theme parks in Orlando. When was your friend clobbered?"

I told him.

"I was right here."

"Your secretary said she couldn't be sure, since she wasn't there."

"That's right. And I didn't have any meetings with anybody. So I've got no alibi, is that what you're saying?"

"Technically, yes."

He snorted. "You don't strike me as stupid. But you're starting to convince me otherwise. Why would I try to hurt Pitts? If I hated him so much, I've had fifty years to do it."

"Some might say you didn't have the opportunity until he showed up."

"I didn't even know he was here."

"Someone could have told you."

He went silent for several seconds. "Listen. I've been patient with you so far. Answered all your questions, even gave you a look at the mine. You're a very foxy lady, and I'd be glad to see you anytime. But from now on, let's keep it on a personal level."

There was a click, then nothing.

I put the phone away, then squinted at the sky.

Another triumph. And the day was just beginning.

* * *

When Stephen came out, I told him about Gant. His jaw dropped. "He said you were *what?*"

"Foxy. I haven't even *heard* that word in at least ten years."

He laughed.

"You know, I don't think he killed Iris," I said.

He leaned against the car. "Why not?"

"He said it himself. Why would he wait fifty years to go after Marvin?"

"Maybe he was afraid the new book would prove the case against his father."

"He doesn't care about his father. The two of them obviously didn't get along."

"That leaves Rose," he said.

I looked down at the gravel. "You already know what I think about that."

"Yeah, and I understand. But what if she really hated her prettier, more popular sister?"

"Enough to kill her? That's insane."

"Hard to believe, yes. But I want to keep an open mind."

"I *have* an open mind. There's a difference between—"

The *1812 Overture* sounded from my pocket. Stephen looked relieved.

It was Sheriff Tanaka.

"Thought you'd want to hear the latest," he said. "No word from the lab on evidence yet. But the official handwriting analysis is back."

He paused as if finding his place on a form. "Says the IRIS sample is too small to make a judgment that would stand up in court."

"You expected that."

"Yeah. But the graphologist added an unofficial comment at the bottom of the report. She says the pressure, speed, and slant used in the pencil drawing are consistent with that used in Sheriff Boyle's signature. And consistent with that typically used by a confident or aggressive individual."

"Really? Well, that's something."

"Maybe, but not something we can use. Too inconclusive."

I wanted to argue but reminded myself I was only an editor.

"Anyway, that's where we are. I'll let you know if there's more."

I was about to hang up when I remembered something. I told him the stoned housekeeper's tale about the shadowy driver of something large. I was afraid he might laugh.

He did. "I'll make a note of it," he said. "But I don't consider the kid a reliable witness, do you?"

"No," I admitted.

When I'd hung up, Stephen looked at me. His eyes were full of questions.

So was my head.

CHAPTER 17

When lunchtime came, we ate sandwiches at a picnic table in Patriots' Park, under the watchful statue of crusading newspaperman Harold P. Trayne. His missing arm and leg had been miraculously restored.

We stared at the aspens, their leaves mostly brown or fallen now, and tolerated the steadily plunging temperature.

Stephen was halfway through his Swiss cheese and tomato when he cleared his throat. "About what I said, keeping an open mind and all that . . ."

"No need to apologize," I said.

"I'm not. Well, I guess I sort of am."

"Don't. You're right to insist on objectivity. If I don't like having only two suspects, I need to find another."

"There aren't any."

"What about Skye?"

He threw up his hands. "Nobody knows who the guy was, much less where he went. He's untraceable, not to mention unidentifiable."

"But what if he *could* be identified?"

"How?"

"The blurry photo doesn't help. But what if he left something else behind, like a fingerprint?"

He finished his sandwich and began to unwrap a brownie. "Where would we find a fingerprint? He lived in a tent. There's no house to search. No car, either. And what did he touch that might have survived for fifty years? A baggie of weed with his name on it?"

"The guy cleared tables at the Pick and Shovel bar, but that's been a thrift store for at least twenty years. What if we could track down, say . . . the glassware, or something else from the saloon, and find a fingerprint on it? It's a long shot, but . . ."

He shook his head. "Too long a shot. Even if we found a print, it could belong to anyone who ever touched the cup or saltshaker or whatever. And how long do fingerprints last, anyway?"

"I don't know. Maybe we should ask the sheriff." I reached in the lunch sack and took out a package of Hostess Sno Balls. Next best thing to doughnuts. I started peeling the marshmallow coating from one, a process that always reminded me of a barbaric attempt at eye surgery.

"Maybe the sheriff is getting tired of us," he said.

"Impossible."

"Well, if he isn't yet, he will be. Nothing personal, but looking for a fingerprint like that is a little desperate."

"Not just a little. It's downright crack-brained. But I see no alternative."

He shrugged. "Just tell him it was *your* idea."

* * *

Twenty minutes later we stood in the sheriff's outer office. He and his deputies were nowhere to be seen.

The dispatcher took off her headset. "If you're looking for

the sheriff, he's at the supermarket. Got a call about a shoplifter. Shouldn't be gone long, if you want to wait."

We sat on two of the three chairs by the door.

"You know," the dispatcher said, lowering her voice, "word's getting around town about you two."

I sat up straight. "What kind of word?"

She glanced toward the front window, as if checking for eavesdroppers. "A few people, including the sheriff, think your book thing sounds sort of exciting. But most of the locals aren't happy about it."

"Why not?"

She shook her head. "Motherlode's been hanging on by its fingernails for the last fifteen years or so. Nobody's ever sure which businesses will reopen in the spring. Most of the restaurants shut down after one or two seasons. Bad publicity about the murder isn't going to help the town's image."

"We've heard that argument before," I said.

"I heard what happened at your motel. You got any protection?"

"You mean a gun?" I asked.

She nodded.

"No. I don't want one."

"The sheriff wouldn't want me saying this, but maybe you should think about it. Or even leave town for a while." She looked at Stephen. "You, too. If it was me, I'd—"

The door opened, and the sheriff walked in.

She put the headset back on and turned away.

I looked at Stephen, who looked at me. "Did she just say what I think she did?" Stephen whispered.

Nodding, I sank into my chair.

* * *

Sheriff Tanaka poured himself a cup of coffee. "Shoplifter, twelve years old," he said to no one in particular. "Gave him a lecture and let him go when his mom showed up."

He took a sip. "What's the matter with these kids? Why stuff half a dozen bottles of Five-Hour Energy Drink in your pocket and try to make it out the front door? So you can stay awake all night and talk on your cellphone?"

It being a rhetorical question, nobody answered.

"Sure hope my kids don't turn out that way." He turned to face us. "Either of you have children?"

"No," we said in unison.

"I recommend having them anyway. Builds character. Anyway, I'm surprised to see you folks here. Seems like we just got off the phone."

"We have a question," I said. "How long do fingerprints last?"

He sat on the edge of Deputy Ponytail's desk. "Afraid I'm not an expert on that subject. Seems to me, though, most prints won't hold up more than a few months, depending on humidity. Pretty dry here, which is good. Paper might work as long as it's not shiny."

He paused for another drink, closing one eye. "I remember reading in one of my evidence courses about somebody getting prints from a piece of Egyptian papyrus using some chemical. You're talking thousands of years there."

He sat there, waiting. "I assume you have a reason for asking."

I explained my idea. Stephen offered no comment, clearly hoping to avoid association with my lunacy.

He scratched his chin. "Interesting." His noncommittal reply made it plain he was used to running for office.

"So," I said, "what personal item made of paper could Skye have touched and left behind?"

"Paper money," Stephen said, apparently deciding to humor me.

"Unlikely," Tanaka said. "Too many people would have handled it—assuming he *had* any money, which he probably didn't."

"A book?" Stephen asked.

I shook my head. "I doubt Skye was much of a reader."

The sheriff finished his coffee and stood up. "Frankly, we could spend all day naming things made out of paper and it wouldn't make a difference. The odds of finding a piece of paper Skye was known to have touched fifty years ago are pretty awful."

He paused. "But if that's how you want to spend your time, more power to you. Meanwhile, I'll wait to get word from the lab on the bit of evidence we collected in your cabin."

I nodded, trying to look grateful and hopeful. But maybe he *was* getting tired of us after all.

As we left, the dispatcher caught my eye. She gave me a look that seemed to say, *Remember what I told you.*

As if I could do otherwise.

CHAPTER 18

WE DROVE TOWARD THE LODGEPOLE INN, CHECKING THE SIDE mirrors more than usual.

"Do you think we need protection?" Stephen asked.

"Not a gun. Though I see nothing wrong with owning one."

"I don't think *anyone* should have a gun," he said. "There. I don't care who knows it."

"Let the record so state. We can debate that another time, when we aren't fearing for our lives."

"What about leaving town?"

I shook my head. "We seem to be making progress. And on a personal note, I'll be fired if the book doesn't sell, which it won't if we don't write it."

"And I'd sure like to get whoever put Marvin in a coma."

"So I say we keep going. Except that I want a baseball bat instead of a toilet plunger next to my bed."

"The dispatcher was exaggerating. Besides, she has a mustache."

I hit the steering wheel with the heel of my hand. "Nothing's going to stop us. I feel like humming the 'Battle Hymn of the Republic.'"

"Please don't," he said.

As we closed in on the Lodgepole Inn, I felt bold as a figurehead on the prow of a Viking ship.

But I kept checking the mirrors.

* * *

About 4:00 p.m. I went to the thrift shop, Second Chances. There seemed to be nowhere else in town that might carry a baseball bat.

Business was sluggish when I got there, even though a sign in the window promised 30% OFF SELECTED ITEMS. I wondered how much longer the store would stay open before winter.

I tried to imagine what it was like in its previous incarnation, the Pick and Shovel tavern where Skye worked. If there was a bar with an oversized painting of a Rubenesque nude in a gold frame, it was long gone. Everything was open and drab and smelled like mothballs.

Since there was no designated sports equipment department, I had to search an aisle at a time. Most of the usual offerings were represented—chipped ceramic cookie jars, scratched plastic laminated end tables, clothing in somebody else's size, books that never should have been published.

But no bats. And nothing made of paper that Skye might have left behind when he quit.

I was about to give up when my phone went off. It was Tracy. I went outside in an alley to take it.

"We're home now," she declared, sounding too tired to celebrate. "Released from the rehab center."

"How is he?"

"A little better every day, which in his case means he's more irritating. I'll put him on."

There was a rustling, then a mischievous voice I hadn't heard in a long time.

"Cranberry! I'm back!"

For a moment I couldn't say anything.

"I mean *really* back. Ask me whatever you want."

I cleared my throat. "Can you remember what you'd discovered before being attacked?"

"Absolutely."

"Hold on." I yanked my notebook and pen from my pocket and prepared to take notes. I tried to use the old brick wall as a desk.

"First of all, I'd just started to uncover the fact that Iris wasn't as pure as the driven snow."

I wrote, but at that angle the pen kept quitting until I shook it. I wondered if NASA was still making those space pens that could write upside-down.

"Fifty years ago," Marvin continued, "nobody talked about stuff like that. At least not in Motherlode, and not where a sainted member of the community was concerned. Iris was kind of like JFK; everybody pretended he wasn't a womanizer, especially after the assassination."

"Uh-huh."

"When I came back to research the update, I went straight to the Historical Museum. It didn't exist fifty years ago. Wanted to see how they treated the murder. Turned out it wasn't mentioned at all. Neither was the book. Kind of ticked me off."

I shook the pen and resumed scribbling.

"The volunteer at the counter, some guy named Keebler, was no help, either. All he did was point me toward George Svoboda, the oldest dude in town. I'd never met George, since fifty years ago he was just some miner with no obvious connection to the case."

He stopped to catch his breath. His brain might be working perfectly now, but he wasn't Superman.

"The old man was careful how he phrased things. But he said something about how people put Iris on a pedestal, that she wasn't as perfect as they made her out to be. I didn't know exactly what he meant, but figured it was worth looking into. I was just starting to find out when *bam*, I got hit."

My pen was skipping so much I could hardly read the result.

"Did you know about Rose MacIlhenny?"

He paused. "Iris's . . . sister?"

"Did you know she still lives in Motherlode?"

"You're kidding."

I told him about Rose and the hatbox.

He whistled. "I didn't know about Hayes, the teacher. But it all fits. Iris got around."

"What does that do to your theory?" I asked.

"Far as I'm concerned, it makes my case against Franklin Gant even stronger. Sheriff Boyle and Hayes probably didn't even know about each other. Gant was the odd man out and couldn't live with it. Kind of an 'If I can't have you, nobody can' thing."

My pen quit.

So did Marvin. "Starting to run out of steam, Cranberry. Not quite a hundred percent yet."

"Of course not."

"We'll talk tomorrow, maybe."

"Sure. Welcome back."

He was silent. When he spoke, there was a catch in his voice. "Thanks for praying. I came that close to never . . ."

I swallowed. I'd never heard him like that.

"Sorry," I said, raising my voice. "The cell service is terrible here. Gotta go."

I hung up, cutting him off.

I knew he'd want it that way.

* * *

Back in the store, I tossed my pen in a trash can and made one more sweep. But there was no bat, and nothing that might have Skye's prints on it.

I was almost out the door when I noticed a battered, heavily taped hockey stick leaning against the wall. There was no price tag.

I asked the cashier, a substantial woman who looked as if she knew her way around the penalty box, how much it was.

"Must've just come in," she said. "Let's say five bucks."

After paying cash, I carried it out.

I set it in the trunk, hoping this weapon would do in a pinch.

Or, better yet, that there would be no pinch at all.

CHAPTER 19

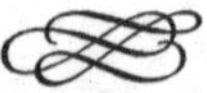

WHEN I TOLD STEPHEN AT DINNER ABOUT MY CONVERSATION with Marvin, he didn't blink once.

"Must have been a pretty emotional experience for both of you," he said.

"A little."

"Well, if he's right, Franklin Gant killed Iris. But that doesn't tell us who slammed Marvin and broke into your cabin. Unless it was Troy."

"But we already agreed he didn't care about defending his—"

"I know. But could he have some other reason for wanting to stop the book?"

I shrugged. "Financial, I suppose. As in reopening the mine. Maybe he's afraid of the same thing the other businesses are—wrecking the town's economy with bad publicity."

"Hard to believe anybody would go to those lengths."

"The dispatcher doesn't seem to think so. And in Gant's case, the mine's his last hope. If he can't get investors, there's no backup plan. He's got a rich boy's standard of living to maintain."

The waitress brought our food, setting Stephen's eyes aflame at the sight of calories and low fiber. Several minutes of unbridled consumption passed before we could return to the subject at hand.

"So Gant has no alibi," he said. "How can we prove he was in Florida, much less in Marvin's office?

"Fingerprints."

He rolled his eyes. "First it's Skye's, now Gant's. Are fingerprints the answer to everything? And how would we get them in the first place?"

"By borrowing something he's touched. Somebody would have to go to his office and get a water bottle or a paper from his desk or something."

He leaned forward. "Well, he seems pretty fond of you."

I set down my fork and raised an index finger. "I see where this is going. I'm not spending ten minutes alone with that guy."

"You could do it in three."

"I take back the idea that we need fingerprints. We'd have nothing to compare them with. The police didn't find any at Marvin's house."

"Maybe he could find some. Now that he's back home, he can dust his whole house if he wants to."

I groaned.

"To quote a very courageous woman," he said, "'Nothing's going to stop us.'"

"I meant—"

"What happened to the 'Battle Hymn of the Republic'? Besides, you can always use your pepper spray."

I looked down at my food. "All right. But if this doesn't work, I'm going to use that spray on *you*."

"You're bluffing. You've got that morality thing going, remember?"

I returned to my eating, but with a lot less gusto.

* * *

When morning came, we drove to the mine.

Neither of us said much, at least for the first five miles.

Finally Stephen turned in my direction. "Your outfit's a bit provocative, don't you think?"

I looked down at my pale yellow blouse and navy blue skirt. "I don't *own* anything provocative. And I'm wearing a coat over it."

"Yeah, but under the circumstances—"

"Besides, isn't provocative what you want? To get this animal so distracted he won't notice when I stuff his computer mouse or whatever in my purse?"

"I withdraw my objection, Your Honor."

We went back to silent mode. The tension was so thick I could have cut it, or him, with a knife.

About 10 minutes later I pulled off the shoulder of the highway before crossing Gant's property line and climbed out. We'd agreed I'd go in alone, so his guard would be down. If I got into trouble, I'd call Stephen on my cell.

Without looking back, I squeezed through the gate and headed for the office. The black SUV was parked there.

I walked through the open entrance. A minute later the door closed.

Gant looked surprised to see me.

"Where's your friend?" he asked, looking wary. He got up and saw the Cruze through the window, then laughed. "Okay, he's technically not on my property. Now, what's this about? Business or pleasure?"

"A little of both."

He shook his head. "We're not goin' down that road. No more questions for your book. If this isn't a personal call, you can take a hike."

"Okay, let's say it's personal."

He smiled. There was a mini-fridge in the corner. He got up, pulled out a half gallon of what looked like orange juice, and filled two paper cups. I figured they were screwdrivers or something, and he wanted to get me drunk. But it tasted like plain old juice.

We talked about the weather, the time he went to Paris and refused to eat snails, and his crazy plans for the mine. The whole time he kept glancing out the window and keeping his eyes off my chest, as if he suspected I had a camera hidden in my hair or something.

After about twenty minutes he looked at his watch. "It's been real," he said. "But I'd better get moving if I'm ever gonna make those dreams come true. Anything else I can do for you?"

I couldn't think of anything. But I hadn't found something that might have his fingerprints on it.

I looked around. Couldn't chance taking his orange juice cup; he'd notice. His desk was piled with papers, though. Calling on all the dramatic ability I could muster, I started to get up, then plopped back in the chair.

"I—I must have altitude sickness," I said. "Could you maybe give me a little more of that juice?"

While his back was turned I grabbed a couple of papers from the nearest stack and stuck them in my coat pocket. I hoped he didn't hear the rustle.

"Here you go," he said. "I'd think you'd be used to the high country by now."

My hand shook a little as I drained the cup. "Guess I . . . had a relapse."

I set the cup down and slowly stood.

"That better?" he asked.

"Much."

"Well, don't be a stranger. And you can tell your friend I don't hold it against him. I'm just done with the past, that's all."

Feeling wobbly as I'd been pretending to be, I walked out the door.

* * *

I climbed into the car. "Drive," I said flatly.

Stephen looked afraid to do otherwise. About three miles later he found the nerve to open his mouth. "What happened?"

When I told him, he whistled in admiration.

"Oh, you're devious," he said, shaking his head.

"That's what you wanted."

"So that's all?" he asked. "No leering glances, no drooling, no groping? By him, I mean."

"Very funny. As a matter of fact, nothing like that happened. After I drank the rest of the juice, he told me to stay hydrated, and I left."

He breathed what sounded like a sigh of relief. "I was so worried. I sat here, wishing I'd brought something to read. Five minutes, then ten. Then fifteen. I checked my phone, and the bars were gone. You couldn't have reached me if your life depended on it."

"Good thing I didn't know that."

"Around the twenty-minute mark I was on the verge of leaping from the car and storming the place. That's when you came out."

Shaking my head, I took Gant's papers from my purse and started to study them.

"*Whoa,*" I said. "Better not cover his fingerprints with yours."

Dropping the sheets in my lap as if they were on fire, I tried to examine them without touching.

"Huh. The first is a past-due bill from the architect who did the renderings of what the reopened mine's supposed to look like. For seven thousand four-hundred dollars."

"So he's in debt already."

"The other's a letter from a lawyer. Threatening to sue if Gant doesn't honor a contract with Copper Ridge Drilling and Excavation."

"There's your motive. Maybe."

I looked up. "Hope he doesn't realize I took these."

Stephen scoffed. "He'll be glad he can't find them. And I'm sure the architect and the lawyer will be happy to send more."

I lifted one page by the edge and slid it into my purse, then did the same with the other.

"Mission accomplished," he said. "I'm glad he didn't . . . well, that nothing happened."

I frowned, then looked down at my outfit. Lowering the visor on my side, I checked myself in the mirror.

"What are you looking at?" he asked.

"Nothing," I said, trying to look nonchalant.

I flipped the visor back up. "Nothing at all."

CHAPTER 20

Treading an already overbeaten path to the sheriff's office, we decided to try his patience again by asking him to analyze the fingerprints on Gant's papers.

The dispatcher saw us first. She looked at us as if to ask why we hadn't left town yet.

Deputy Crabb, meanwhile, regarded us with suspicion. "If you're looking for the sheriff, he's not here. He's at a political fundraiser in Copper Ridge."

Reaching into my purse, I gingerly withdrew the two sheets of paper. Holding them by their margins, I dropped them on his desk.

"These could be a break in the MacIlhenny case," I said. "We're hoping you can dust them for fingerprints, or whatever it is you do, and tell us whether they belong to Troy Gant."

He frowned, his freckled face making him look like a petulant child. "How did you get these documents?"

We told him, more or less. The part about the orange juice seemed extraneous, so we skipped it.

He shook his head. "These can't be used in court. They

were obtained without a search warrant. The chain of evidence has already been broken. The Sheriff's Department can't have anything to do with them."

"But it wouldn't have to be used in court. If they're his prints, you could get official ones later."

He shook his head. *"Everything* the Sheriff's Department does is official." He pulled the metal wastebasket from under his desk, then fished a used FedEx envelope out of it. "Here. You can use this to take the sheets with you."

"But—"

"Godspeed," he said.

I sighed. Carefully Stephen picked up the papers. I held the envelope open so he could slide them in.

Defeated, we walked out the door.

We paused on the other side. "Too bad we didn't get the other deputy instead," Stephen said.

I waved the envelope at nothing in particular. "No. This will not stand."

"Excuse me?"

"I went to a lot of trouble to get these prints. Too much trouble."

Pivoting, I proceeded to march back inside. Stephen followed, probably hoping we weren't about to find ourselves behind the bars of that little cell.

The dispatcher's eyes widened when she saw us. Deputy Crabb stood up.

"Forget something?"

I took off my coat and placed it on a chair. "I did. I forgot how much I have to learn about . . . things you probably know so much about." I tried to keep my voice sounding like warm butter, or at least margarine.

He narrowed one eye. "What kind of things?"

"Like how to get fingerprints. I've always wanted to know how to do that."

"Ms. . . . Neville, was it?"

"Carolyn."

"We're not running a school here. I can't take time to teach you anything. Try a Law Enforcement course at a community college."

I nodded. "I can see how busy you are. I don't know how you get it all done. But it would only take a couple of minutes, and then I can take it from there." I stepped closer. "I'll do the rest for you."

He cleared his throat. "Well, I . . . if it'll mean you'll stop interrupting . . ."

"I promise."

He scratched his chin. "Just a minute." He went into the back room.

The dispatcher frowned, shaking her head.

He returned with a small, flat white jar and a gray, hypodermic-sized gadget with a plunger on the end. "Most civilians don't know about magnetic fingerprint powder," he said.

He tore a page from his desk calendar and turned it over. "Press your thumb on this a few times."

I went to the desk, leaned toward him as far as modesty would allow, and mashed the paper repeatedly. He backed up a step, looking flustered.

"I . . . okay, good." After unscrewing the lid of the jar, he picked up the gray thing. "Now we get the powder." He pushed the plunger into the jar. When he lifted it, a fuzzy-looking black clump clung to it.

"Magnetic iron filings," he said. "Now we drag them slowly over the paper." He dangled the plunger over the sheet, barely touching it. "You have to be very gentle. Like a feather."

"You obviously know what you're doing," I said, my voice awash in awe.

Sure enough, my ghostly prints began to take shape.

He held the plunger over the jar and pressed. The black cluster fell back in.

"And that's all there is to it," he said.

"May I try?"

"Well, okay." He handed me the plunger.

Cautiously I withdrew the two sheets from the FedEx envelope. I fished a clump of iron filings from the jar and dragged them over the first sheet, then the second.

"My gosh," I said. "Look at that."

I leaned over the pages. Faint, overlapping images could be seen at the margins of both.

"I don't know whose they are," I said. "But they're there." I turned to the deputy. "I don't suppose you'll change your mind about—"

He shook his head. "I'll take those iron filings, though." He held the jar under the plunger, and I let them go.

Stephen held the envelope open while I slipped the pages back in.

"Thank you, Deputy," I said. "You've been more helpful than you know."

Straightening up, he reverted to his usual censorious expression. "The rest is up to you," he said.

A few moments later we stood in front of the office. "I'm not sure what we have here," Stephen said.

I, on the other hand, was pretty satisfied. It had nothing to do with fingerprints.

* * *

At lunch I insisted on keeping the envelope by my side in our booth. "We need a safe place for this," I said.

"Where would you suggest?"

"Not the motel. Certainly not my cabin, and probably not

yours." Despite my newly acquired hockey stick, the place seemed as secure as an open field.

"A safe deposit box?" he asked.

"As far as I know, there's only one bank in this town. It's about the size of a three-car garage."

He took out his phone and found the web page. "Mountain View Savings and Loan." He punched in the number.

"Hi. Do you have safety deposit boxes?" He paused, listening. "Oh. Well, never mind." He pushed the END button.

"They're reserved for account holders," he said. "And there's a six-month waiting list."

I pushed away my empty plate. "How about the Historical Museum? It has bars on some of the windows. But we'd never get it past Keebler."

"We need a place with an alarm system." He thought for a moment. "Like Rose's shop."

"Are you kidding? Did you see how she looked at me last time we were there?"

"We're going to find a place for these prints. Leave Rose to me."

When we finished our lunch, he put the envelope under his arm. As we headed for the car, I heard him humming the Battle Hymn.

* * *

A new sign hung in the window at Rose's. It said END OF SEASON SALE, not to be confused with PRE-INVENTORY SALE.

The place was busier than ever. "Maybe we should come back another time," I said.

"You wish. We're staying put. Let me do the talking."

I passed the time by pretending to examine the nearest piece of merchandise, which happened to be a radio shaped like a moose. Apparently you could adjust the volume by turning its shaggy head, and the frequency by twisting its antlers. I made a mental note not to get one.

When we finally got Rose's attention, she smiled at Stephen. She acknowledged me with a nod I couldn't interpret.

"We're looking at one of these rock tables," Stephen said, waving toward the ugliest of three on display. "Carolyn tells me they're made by George Svoboda."

"That's right," Rose said.

A small sign sat on the table: WAS $249, NOW $199.

I nearly gagged. This particular creation, featuring a phony-looking chunk of mint-jelly-green agate floating in the center like a slice of decaying ham, wasn't one of Mr. Svoboda's best efforts.

"We'll take it," Stephen said.

My jaw dropped. I hadn't planned to spend $200 on anything today, much less something that looked like it had pulled a C in remedial shop class. Not to mention that I had no way to get it back to Connecticut, which, come to think of it, I didn't want to do anyway.

I opened my mouth to protest, but Stephen cut me off with a look. I had, after all, agreed to let him do the talking.

Rose waved to her teenage employee, who was two aisles away. "Dax, can you help load this?"

"In a minute," he called, sweeping up something broken.

"Rose," Stephen said, "do you have an alarm system here?"

"Yes. Why do you ask?"

Holding up the envelope, he lowered his voice. "We have some really important fingerprints here. They could be from the person who broke into Carolyn's cabin. Maybe even the one who attacked Marvin. Could we leave them here for a while?"

Rose turned to me. "So, are these *my* fingerprints?"

"No. In fact, they're from fingers that point to someone else. So to speak."

She nodded. "I have a fireproof box in the back, if the envelope isn't too big."

Her office was no bigger than a cubicle at Pendleton House, crammed with as many cartons and stacks of paper as the average warehouse. On the wall hung a poster of a tranquil rain forest, probably a vain effort to overcome the chaos.

The fireproof box was in the closet, on the floor. She got down on her hands and knees, unlocked it, and placed the envelope inside. "It fits. Just barely."

She got to her feet, then smiled. "Come back anytime to visit your evidence locker."

"Thank you," Stephen said.

Back on the sales floor, Dax rang up our misguided purchase. I tried not to look at the total on the credit card reader, knowing that for the price of this eyesore I could have had three moose radios.

Stephen and the young man gripped opposite ends of the table and wrestled it into the trunk with a lot of grunting and testosterone. Sadly, it fit.

Stephen was already in the car when I slid behind the wheel. "I thought compliments were the way to a woman's heart," I said. "Not money."

He shook his head. "You tried that, remember? Time to go for broke."

I turned the key in the ignition.

Broke, I thought. How appropriate.

At this rate, it would soon be the perfect choice of words.

CHAPTER 21

WE HAULED THE TABLE BACK TO THE LODGEPOLE INN, listening to it shift and thunk.

"What are we supposed to do with it?" I asked.

"Let's bring it inside for now."

"To your cabin, not mine."

He shook his head. "Wouldn't be right. You paid for it. You should get the benefits."

"Which are?"

"Knowing you've supported small business, the backbone of our economy."

We managed to pry it out and lug it inside. Stephen seemed determined not to make any noise betraying the strain, apparently unwilling to admit his idea had been ill-advised. The monstrosity was, after all, just big enough to get in the way and just small enough to have no practical value.

Flopping into a chair, I stared at the table as one might regard an especially difficult child.

He sat down, too, trying not to sound breathless. "Tell me more about . . . the guy who made this thing."

"George is quite a character. When I went to his place, he—"

My phone started ringing. I fished it out.

It was Marvin. Marvin himself, without Tracy's help. I put him on speaker.

"Good news, Cranberry. I'm completely back to normal."

"Are you sure that's a good thing?"

"Got cabin fever, girl. Absolutely ready to come to Colorado, but Tracy won't let me. Claims I need more time to recover."

"She's probably right. The air's pretty thin."

"Then tell me what's going on."

I updated him, mostly on the search for Skye, Gant's motive, and the fingerprints of both.

"Honey, you're obsessed with fingerprints."

"That's what they tell me."

"Probably your only chance of finding Skye's print is to find a book he owned."

Stephen leaned in. "That's what *I* thought."

"But people don't read books anymore," I countered. "Much less own them."

"We're talking about fifty years ago. Even hippies were reading, at least when they weren't too wasted. Stuff like *Siddhartha* and *The Hobbit*."

"I'll take your word for it. If you find out whether Skye owned a book, let me know."

"I'll tell you in person." He lowered his voice. "Anytime now, I'll make it back out there."

"Over my dead body!" Tracy yelled in the background.

"Better go. I'll call when I get a chance. But we probably don't need to do the daily thing anymore."

"Fine with me. What matters is that you and Tracy are okay."

There was a pause. "God bless," he said, and hung up.

* * *

I set the phone on the rock table.

"You were telling me about George Svoboda," Stephen said.

"Oh. Well, when I went to his place, he gave me quick descriptions of some people involved with the MacIlhenny case. He may be the only one who remembers Skye. Not that he wants to."

"They didn't get along?"

"As far as I know, they never said a word to each other. But George saw how he operated. Called Skye 'the drug boy.' Smelled like incense, he said. Remembered how Skye was always quoting hippie poetry by some communist prophet."

He looked puzzled. "Since when do communists have prophets?"

"Probably just George's way of saying the man was religious. Or that he predicted the future."

"So who was he?"

"No idea."

He tilted his head to one side. "Was Nostradamus big back then?"

"Mister doom and gloom. Too depressing. Anyone who read him wouldn't have smiled all the time."

"What about those maharishis in India? With the scraggly hair?"

I shook my head. "Most people called them gurus. Holy men. Or fakes. But not prophets."

He leaned forward. "Wasn't there a guy who wrote a book called *The Prophet?* Name starts with a J. Or a G."

"Gibran? Khalil Gibran?"

"I'm not old enough to know this stuff. I have to rely on you."

"Hey, I missed the sixties by about fifteen years. But I

know Gibran specialized in claptrap. It might seem like wisdom if you were under the influence. I've read just enough of his sayings to know I don't want to read any more. Probably the most likely candidate."

"Care to share a few quotes?"

"Don't remember any. But I can see the cover of the edition I checked out of the college library. Yellow, with kind of an eerie, smeary pencil sketch of a face that looked like a death mask. I brought the book back long before it was due."

"Wow. The ultimate bad review."

"Skye probably had his own copy. Memorized half of it. Maybe even carried it around with—"

I stopped.

"What?"

My heart beat a little faster. "*The Prophet*," I said. "If Skye owned a book, that could be the one."

"So what happened to it?"

"I have no idea. I also have no idea how to find out."

"Well, that's a good start." Yawning, he checked his watch and stood up. "Maybe it'll come to you in a dream. 'Night."

When he was gone, I went back to staring at the rock table. It seemed, after all, to have no other use.

Especially when you had to regain your strength and get ready to do the impossible.

CHAPTER 22

It came to me over a waffle the next morning. I had nobody to share my eureka moment with, though, as Stephen was sleeping in. Apparently lifting the rock table had worn him out.

To find out whether Skye had left a copy of *The Prophet* with anyone, we needed to know who his friends in Motherlode had been. The problem, of course, was that nobody knew. At least nobody we'd met.

There was that photo, the blurry group shot at the bar. Skye wasn't part of the group, little more than a blob in the background. But was there a way to identify the others? Might some of his companions have been caught by the camera, too?

I finished the waffle, downed the last of my coffee, walked to my cabin, and waited.

When Stephen finally knocked on my door, I told him about my epiphany.

"Huh," he said. "Can't hurt to try, I guess."

I shuttled us to the sheriff's office. Tanaka was back, pouring himself a coffee.

The dispatcher wasn't at her desk. Neither was Deputy Ponytail.

But Deputy Crabb sat at his, filling out what was undoubtedly some kind of report. He didn't look up, probably embarrassed that in a moment of weakness he'd fallen prey to my powers of persuasion.

When I'd laid out my theory that Skye might have owned a copy of *The Prophet*, the sheriff took a long swallow from his cup. "Never heard of that book," he said.

"You're a lucky man," I said. "Is there a way to find out whether Skye had the book and left it with anyone? Who his friends were when he was here? Maybe using the photo?"

He looked confused for a moment. "The one in the file?" He went to the cabinet, rolled out the drawer, and tossed the picture on his desk. "Good luck with that. I can barely make the guy out."

I picked up the print. "But there are plenty of other people. Including a few employees. Could anyone identify them?"

He shook his head. "The owner of that bar is long gone. And if you're thinking of old George, I'm sure he didn't hang with that crowd. Even if he could see well enough to tell who they were."

"But—"

"I'm afraid you're barking up the wrong tree, Ms. Neville. You'd do a lot better to look at the list."

"List?"

He pulled the folder from the drawer. "Remember how Sheriff Boyle hated all the druggies and ski bums who came through here? Blamed them for everything, including the MacIlhenny murder. He made that little list of Skye's 'associates.' You probably saw it in the file."

He placed the single page on his desk. "Never gave it much thought. Figured it was just part of his paranoia."

I stepped forward to look it over, and Stephen followed. Seven names, none of which I recognized. No addresses, no phone numbers.

"Not much to go on," he said. "But I'll make you a copy."

He did, then handed it to me. "Knock yourself out."

"I'm sure she will," Stephen said. "And she'll make me do the same."

I slipped the page into my pocket. *Getting closer,* I thought.

I just didn't know what we were getting closer to.

* * *

RODNEY JANEWAY
MARIA CARTENA
ALTHEA LIGHTNER
RUSSELL BOSCH
JIMMY FIELDS
KIKI UNTERMEYER
HONG HANH NGUYEN

Sitting in Stephen's cabin, we stared at the names. The list was a gauntlet, flung down at our feet.

"Where do we start?" Stephen asked, fingers poised over his laptop keyboard.

"At the beginning."

He launched his browser, but the screen said YOU ARE NOT CONNECTED TO THE INTERNET.

"Crap," he said. After quitting, he tried again. This time, for reasons unknown, it worked.

For the next 95 minutes the tenuous connection kept dropping, then mysteriously relinking. We learned there are far too many people in the world, and that most of them need to change their names to avoid duplication.

We also discovered that Rodney Janeway was deceased. So was Maria Cartena. And Kiki Untermeyer, who didn't sound old enough to die of natural causes—but had anyway.

Russell Bosch had vanished mysteriously, in the sense that the Internet had never made his acquaintance. The same was true of Hong Hanh Nguyen, unless she'd somehow managed to live here and in Riverhead, New York at the same time.

That left Althea Lightner and Jimmy Fields. The former was said to reside in Copper Ridge. The latter lived somewhere near Motherlode.

I wrote down Althea's address. But before I could record Jimmy's, the wi-fi cut out and refused to reconnect.

"Crap again," Stephen said. "Maybe Edna can help us."

"Who?"

"The vulture at the front desk."

"You mean the Cranky Old Woman."

"Right."

We made our way to the office and buzzed.

This time we smelled her before we saw her. It was the scent of Vicks VapoRub, that piercing menthol whose function seemed to be warding off anyone who might be sicker than you are.

Her sweater of the day, pulled more tightly than ever, was a rare shade of green, somewhere between pea soup and poison ivy.

"We've lost our Internet," I said sweetly.

The old woman grunted. "Told you that would happen." Oddly, she didn't sound congested or hoarse or anything other than loathsome. Maybe she just liked to repel people.

"Is there anything you can do?" Stephen asked.

"You kidding? It's those clowns at Greater Mountain

Internet. And the Rocky Mountains. You expect me to move 'em?"

"Not today," I said. "Do you know a man named Jimmy Fields?"

She cackled, but not as endearingly as Marvin was known to do. "Yeah, everybody knows Jimmy."

"We're trying to find out where he lives," I said.

She snorted. "It's no secret. Outside of town. Take Auchincloss Road about five miles. Can't miss it."

"Why can't you miss it?" I asked.

She gave a hollow laugh. "You'll see."

Turning, she plodded into whatever twisted world lay behind her door.

All that remained was the smell.

* * *

After lunch we took the road out of town, further up the mountain. Nobody else seemed to be going our way.

Every so often the march of evergreens would part to reveal a meadow, dotted with gray boulders and grass the color of straw. In the shadows I could see frost.

Soon the pavement ended, fading into gravel. The grade steepened. Slowing, the Cruze labored upward.

"It's a different world up here," Stephen said.

I kept an eye on the temperature gauge. "One this car isn't meant for. Should have rented something made for Colorado, not Manhattan. We don't have snow tires, let alone chains."

Another meadow unfolded, this one strewn with heaps of dark brown rotting wood, the tumbledown ruins of old miner's cabins. A green and white State of Colorado sign by the road warned visitors not to take souvenirs.

"Who would *want* this stuff?" Stephen asked.

"It's historical. Rusty old bean cans. Square nails. Blue glass patent medicine bottles."

"Oh. When you put it that way, I can understand the attraction."

We climbed higher. My ears popped. Eventually a weathered split-rail fence began to unwind along the road. A jumble of objects were nailed to it—hub caps, aluminum pie plates, corroded gears the size of wall clocks, yellow sunflower pinwheels.

A flock of plastic pink flamingos congregated just inside the fence, followed by a couple of bears carved with chainsaws and a family of lawn gnomes. Then a line of faded flags that looked as if they'd come from a garage sale at the United Nations.

Finally we saw a shack with a tin roof and two totem poles in the yard. And, for some reason, a giant white fiberglass toilet that seemed to belong on a miniature golf course.

"So this is what Edna was talking about," Stephen said.

I parked the car on the shoulder. The engine fan kept running.

There was a gate made of bedsprings in the fence, but it was unlocked.

"I've never seen anything quite like this," Stephen said.

"You weren't raised in Idaho."

We made our way toward the water-stained door. When I knocked, a dog began to bark inside.

Finally the door opened. We squinted through the screen.

Jimmy Fields was big in all directions. A bristly white mustache drooped to his chin like a feather boa. Combat fatigues and boots made up his outfit, along with a discolored leather outback hat on a mostly bald head.

The dog was at his feet, still barking and clicking his nails on the floor and looking even more menacing in person. I'm not familiar with all the breeds, but I think he was an ox.

"Major!" Jimmy yelled. "Shut your face!" The animal ignored him.

Jimmy blinked at us as if he'd just awakened. "Yeah?"

I explained why we'd come, leaving out practically everything except the parts about Skye being a friend of his and our questions about the book. I hoped he could hear me over the barking.

Finally the dog shut up. "Come on in," Jimmy said.

The place stank of fried fish, wet dog, and what could only be marijuana.

When we sat down, he claimed a round wicker chair with an orange pillow. Stephen and I took a gray vinyl sofa that seemed to have been on the losing end of a knife fight.

Our host didn't offer refreshments, which was a relief. I guessed we'd have required antibiotics immediately afterward.

The dog trotted over and began to nuzzle at Stephen's crotch. Jimmy seemed not to notice, but I stifled a laugh. "Major likes you," I said.

He pushed the beast away, a tough thing to do without touching him. "Have I ever told you how much I hate dogs?" he whispered.

"No, but it doesn't surprise me."

Jimmy stared blankly at us. "What was it you wanted again?"

When I launched into a recap, it was with considerably less detail than the first time.

"Wow," Jimmy said. "I haven't seen Skye since . . . whenever it was. We had some good times. I think we did, anyway."

"What was he like?" I asked.

"Most mellow person I ever met, at least in the beginning. Always quoting that prophet guy. Never saw him read a book, though."

I leaned forward. "When you say he was mellow in the beginning, what do you mean?"

He smoothed his mustache with a beefy hand. A little smile escaped as he did so. "We used a lot of weed, a little coke. Hardly ever coke. Out of our price range. I stopped there, but he dropped acid a few times. You know, LSD."

"Lysergic acid diethylamide," Stephen said, showing off.

"He said the first time was very spiritual. But he kind of changed after that. Joked about hearing voices. At least he said he was joking. Then he was gone, after that teacher died. Nobody knew if there was a connection, or where he went."

Leaning back, I crossed my legs. "Do you think he could have killed Iris?"

He grunted. "Don't think so. But you never know. I didn't think a lot of things were possible, either. Until the Battle of Khe Sanh."

There was a long silence.

"What did you do after the war?" I asked gently.

"Oh, I worked in the mine for a while. Hurt my back. Been on disability for . . . well, however long it's been."

The dog was back, no doubt with a new tank of saliva. Stephen stood up, leaving him with nothing to nuzzle.

"I think we'll be moving along," I said.

"Suit yourself." He didn't get up.

"Do you recall a woman named Althea Lightner?" I asked.

He flipped through his mental Rolodex, which was apparently missing a lot of cards.

"Was that his girlfriend?"

"We think so. She lives in Copper Ridge."

"Huh. Skinny chick. Followed Skye around like a lost puppy. You should ask *her* this stuff."

"We plan to," I said. "Thanks for your time."

"Hey," he said. "Time's all I got."

We saw ourselves out, then past the totem poles and the gargantuan toilet. I held the bedspring gate open for Stephen.

He shook his head. "Ever see that old TV commercial with the fried egg that said, 'This is your brain on drugs?'"

"Yeah. Pretty sad."

The gate shut behind me with a rusty creak.

"Six down, one to go," I said. "For your sake, I hope Althea Lightner doesn't have a dog."

And, more importantly, that she had a few little gray cells left.

CHAPTER 23

Next morning we reunited at the Ore Cart. It was later than usual, the alarm clocks at the Lodgepole Inn being no more reliable than the wi-fi. Only two tables were occupied, probably because the summer crowd was all but gone. The waitress seemed to come by every five minutes, trying to use up the coffee.

"I think you should get a cat," I said, working on my vegetarian omelet.

Stephen refused to look up from his blueberry muffin and Canadian bacon. "I think I've made my position on pets clear."

"But you have so much in common with cats. They're aloof, couldn't care less what anyone thinks, insist on having things their way, don't put up with change . . ."

He smiled a fake smile. "Let's talk about Althea Lightner. Should we call her or just show up?"

"Well, we don't know how she feels about Skye now. And what if she's married and never told her husband about him? She won't be able to say much." I checked my watch. "It's late enough that she's probably up."

We finished our meal, then went to the car. After dialing I put the call on speaker.

A man answered. *Uh-oh,* I thought.

"Mr. Lightner?" I said.

"Who's calling?" He sounded wary.

I told him my name. "I'm in Motherlode right now, but I work for Pendleton House Publishers in New York. I'm trying to reach Althea."

"What about?"

"We're writing a book about this town, and we'd like to ask her how it was in the 1960s."

"Oh. Well, okay. Hang on." There was a pause, then a distant shout. "Allie! Phone!"

"Hello?"

Her voice was breathy, surprisingly girlish. She was, after all, at least 70.

Stephen and I took turns explaining the usual. The more we said, the more interested she sounded.

Until I mentioned Skye.

After a pause, she lowered her voice. "We'll need to meet somewhere. Not here."

"We'll come to you," I said.

"The public library's near my house. They have meeting rooms."

"What time?"

She paused. "Eleven o'clock?"

We got the address, then hung up.

Stephen looked out his window. "I guess that answers the question of whether she's told her husband about Skye."

I put the phone away. "But the real question isn't answered yet."

"What's that?"

"How much will she tell us?"

* * *

The North Branch of the Copper Ridge Public Library System was one of those places with hardly any books in it, designed for those who didn't read by those who wanted desperately to please them.

On the main floor we passed a coffee shop and snack bar where shelves should have been, a cavelike room of beanbag chairs and video games to coax errant juveniles from the streets, and computers on which homeless derelicts could watch free Internet porn. Upstairs was a Creators' Lab with a 3D printer, DVDs, a performance stage for townspeople to recite bad poetry, and an invisible collection of e-books.

I shook my head. "No doubt this was subsidized by the same government agency that sponsors pickleball courts."

Stephen ignored me. We'd had this conversation before, and as a millennial he was insufficiently alarmed.

There were three meeting rooms, A, B, and C. We stood outside C, waiting, having no idea what sort of female septuagenarian to look for. I imagined an aging child of nature, tie-dyed or peasant-dressed or wreathed in something gauzy.

At 11:08, she proved me wrong. Approaching us, ducking her head as if trying to avoid attention, she looked like a member of the school board. Clad in a navy blue pantsuit, she was a bit on the plump side and had a grandmotherly gray perm into which no daisies had been stuck.

"Are you the folks from New York?" she asked. Her voice was still breathy, but now more hushed than girlish.

We nodded.

"Room B," she said. After leading us in, she made sure the door was closed all the way.

"Wow," Stephen said, looking out the window. "That's quite a view."

Downtown Copper Ridge seemed determined to be as

little like Motherlode as possible. There were traffic lights, speed limit signs, bike paths, and even a four-story office building which, if it did not scrape the sky, at least aspired to.

We sat at a round table. "So you knew Skye," I said.

She nodded.

"Did you know his last name?"

She shook her head. "He never told me. It didn't seem necessary. Quite a few people had one-word names like that in those days."

"So," I said. "Tell us about—"

"First things first," Althea said, looking worried. "I love my husband. We've been happily married for thirty-nine years. We've raised two wonderful children."

I waited for the rest, but in vain.

"Congratulations," I said. "But what about Skye?"

She sighed. "Even now, I've never known anyone quite like him. I can't imagine spending my life with him, of course. But I can't forget him, either."

"I take it you haven't told your husband about him."

"Don? No. And I'm not planning to. He doesn't need to know."

"How would you describe your relationship?"

"We were only together about two months. I was home from college for the summer, and my parents lived in Denver. I waitressed part-time at the Pick and Shovel. That's where we met. When Skye wasn't working, we'd take long walks. He loved hiking, which was probably why he was such a beanpole."

"What else did you do?" I asked.

"Ate a lot of brown rice and carrot juice, along with this whole-wheat bread that was so heavy we could have built chimneys with it." She looked out the window. "And spent several nights in his tent. The sheriff said later that he was some kind of drug addict, but we never did more than a little pot."

"Would you call him . . . a spiritual person?"

"Oh, yes. What attracted me most was his spirit. The way he gave you permission to be as free as he was. He loved to quote all these people. Like Lao Tzu. And Khalil Gibran."

The hair on the back of my neck stood up.

"Did he have Gibran's book? *The Prophet*?"

"Of course. Kept it in his backpack."

My heart rate jumped.

"Do you know what happened to it?"

"He gave it to me a few days before he left."

I swallowed. "I don't suppose you still have it."

"In a box in the garage. It's full of highlighting and a few notes. It just didn't seem right to get rid of it."

"Could we . . . borrow it?"

"Whatever for?"

I told her why. I wanted to skip the part about how her ex-boyfriend might be a killer, but couldn't find a way around it.

"You think he strangled that poor girl? No way. Skye couldn't have murdered anybody."

"If that's so, the fingerprints will prove it. You've got nothing to worry about."

She sank into her chair. "I can't get tangled up in this. Don will find out."

I folded my hands on the table. "What would Don think if he knew you wouldn't help find that poor girl's killer?"

She winced.

"No one will find out unless those are Skye's prints," I said. "If they are, your husband will see that you did the right thing."

Althea closed her eyes for a long time. Finally she opened them and sighed.

"I guess I can live with that. I'm pretty sure Skye's gone by now, so it won't make any difference to him. He wasn't quite meant for this world, you know?"

I nodded. "Oh, one other thing. You remember Jimmy Fields? He was another friend of Skye's."

She frowned, thinking. "I don't . . . oh, wait. A big guy?"

"Definitely."

"I might have met him once, but that's it."

"He's still alive. Lives outside Motherlode. Not in very good shape, though."

"Wow. I had no idea where he went."

"He thinks Skye used LSD. Did you ever see any signs he'd had a bad trip or heard voices?"

She shook her head. "People said he smiled all the time. As far as I could tell, he really did."

I looked at Stephen. "Any other questions?"

"Um . . . no."

"Althea, would it be possible to borrow that book today?"

"Well, yes, but we'd have to go back to my house."

"We'll follow you."

"But Don will be there."

I thought for a moment. "We can park down the block. You could bring it to us."

She nodded, stood, and took a last look through the window.

"We were all so young then," she said, and walked out the door.

* * *

We were halfway back to Althea's house when Stephen suddenly sat up straight. "I just thought of something," he said. "The fingerprints."

"What about them?"

"We can't just get Skye's. Althea's prints are probably all over that book, too. We'll need hers to distinguish them."

"How do we do that?"

"I saw an episode of *Castle* once where he took some with Scotch tape. Or maybe it was *Bones*. No, probably not *Bones*. Skeletons don't have prints."

"I don't have any Scotch tape, do you?"

"Of course not. I hope *she* does."

When we got to Althea's street, she turned into her driveway. Her husband's car was still there. I kept going, slowly, and parked at the end of the block.

About 10 minutes later she emerged from the house, carrying her purse. After spotting us, she came our way.

I lowered my window. Her face was pink, and her forehead looked moist.

"I got it as fast as I could. It wasn't in the box I thought it was in."

She reached into her purse and handed me the book. It was the same edition I remembered, a mass market paperback, the corners worn smooth and the spine cracked.

"Please take good care of it," she said.

With my finger I drew an X over my heart. "You'll get it back, we promise."

"Do you have any Scotch tape?" I asked.

"The wide kind," Stephen added.

"Tape? Why?"

When I explained, Althea made an exasperated noise. "I'll be back."

A few minutes later, she was. "Don is starting to wonder what's going on. I hope we can make this quick."

"Come around to my side," Stephen said, rolling down his window. "Good. Now hold out your hands."

He tore off a bit of tape, pressed it against the woman's thumb, and sealed it with a second strip. After repeating the process for each digit of her right hand, he slipped the strips into her pocket.

"Thank you," I said. "We'll be in touch."

She was already walking away as quickly as she could.

I pulled the Cruze away from the curb. Stephen cradled the book in his lap.

"I'm afraid to open it," he said.

"Good. Don't."

We headed toward the highway, guarding the little paperback as if it were the key to everything.

Because it very well might be.

* * *

On the way out of town just after noon, we stopped at McDonald's and Wal-Mart, both of them ineffectively camouflaged with cedar and green paint to look like they belonged in a mountain village. Stephen refused to enter, citing his philosophical opposition to corporate greed.

After walking past a disgustingly premature Halloween display and seeing no one with whom to register a complaint, I bought a package of 10 disposable white latex gloves. When I returned to the car, Stephen asked what they were for.

I handed him the bag. "Let's slide the book in here," I said. "We'll need the gloves later, for handling it." He looked relieved when our precious cargo was sealed and stowed in the back seat, no longer in his custody.

By the time we reached the Lodgepole Inn, Stephen was in Hitting the Wall mode.

"I know it's only the middle of the afternoon," he said, climbing unsteadily from the car. "But I'm going to crash. Maybe watch a little basic cable."

I took the bag from the back seat. "Don't you want to see what we've got here?"

"Later." He trudged toward Cabin Eight.

As soon as I entered Cabin Six, I fished the latex glove 10-pack from the bag and gouged it open with my thumb. The gloves looked flimsy. Carefully I pulled one over each hand.

I took a deep breath, then withdrew the book. It seemed even more fragile than it had at first.

Trying to touch only the edges, I opened it slowly. There was a handwritten message—block letters, not longhand, in blue ballpoint pen. The ink hadn't faded, but the characters looked hurried, slapdash:

To the Lovely Althea
Run toward the Light

S.

I flipped ahead a few pages. Comments crowded the margins every so often, nearly indecipherable. Seemingly random passages were underlined or highlighted, the yellow of the marker barely discernible thanks to fading ink and the acid in the paper. The notes were mostly exclamations of agreement, like *Yes!* and *So true!* and *!!!!!!!!!*

My heart thumped. We had more than fingerprints here. We had samples of Skye's handwriting, too.

Jumping forward to a section on love, I read the following gaseous declaration from the Prophet:

Love gives naught but itself and takes naught but from itself.
Love possesses not nor would it be possessed;
For love is sufficient unto love.

It was followed by this comment: *The Earth moves when you move the Earth.* It must have meant something to Skye, but my state was apparently too unaltered to appreciate it.

I examined a few more pages, unable to stand only so much wisdom in one sitting, then slipped the book back into the bag. After peeling the gloves off with a snap I sat there, not bothering to wipe the crooked grin off my face.

We'd found the unfindable.

I hadn't felt this successful since I'd signed that former First Lady to write a children's book about her parakeet. It had ended up losing a great deal of money, but for one shining moment victory had been mine.

Something told me this triumph would be just as permanent.

CHAPTER 24

By morning, Stephen was recharged. In fact, he was in Overdrive. The three cups of coffee he drank at the Ore Cart only made things worse.

We went to the sheriff's office again, bringing the book.

This time a racket reached our ears before we got through the door.

Tanaka was swinging the holding cell door shut on a thirtyish drunk in denim and a puffy vest. The man gripped the bars, belting out "Sloop John B." He wailed the loudest every time he came to the phrase, *Let me go home.*

The dispatcher also was fully engaged, taking a call from Deputy Ponytail, who apparently had encountered a dead deer on the highway. Hearing that news, Stephen looked desolate, thanks to his empathy with wildlife and all that caffeine.

"You folks need something?" the sheriff called over the din.

I held up the book bag. "Could we convene in your office?" I asked.

He looked around as if to make sure things would be safe without him. “I guess so.”

After shutting the door behind him, he cleared his throat. “I’m glad the Beach Boys aren’t here to see this.”

“We have the book,” I said. “The one Skye left behind.”

“No, really?”

“He gave it to his girlfriend, and she loaned it to us. He not only touched it, he wrote in it.”

“I’m impressed.”

“Can you get someone to examine it for prints?”

He scratched the side of his nose. “I can send it to the Colorado Bureau of Investigation in Lakewood. They do a fine job, but it takes a while.”

“We’re beggars, not choosers.”

“Now, there’s a complication. The girlfriend probably left as many prints as Skye did. Will she give us hers, too?”

“She already did,” Stephen said, reaching into his pocket and holding up his open palm.

“What have you got there?” Tanaka asked.

“We got her fingerprints on Scotch tape.”

The sheriff laughed, then rummaged through the top drawer of his desk and found an envelope. “Put ’em in here. We can get real prints later for court, if this gets that far.”

He turned to me. “And you can hand me that book.”

I picked up the bag. “I’m a little concerned about sending it through the mail. Anything could happen.”

“You don’t trust the Postal Service?”

“Does anyone?”

He shook his head. “We’ll send it FedEx Overnight.”

On the way out we passed the holding cell. The drunk had stopped caterwauling and was passed out on a cot.

Stephen looked at me. “You know who the Beach Boys are, right?” he asked.

I rolled my eyes. "If you have to ask, you don't know me at all," I said, and kept walking.

* * *

The second we stepped outside, the cold hit us like a summons. Shivering despite my overcoat, I squinted at the clouds.

"No snow yet," Stephen said. "But they said on TV that an 'old-fashioned Colorado winter' could start anytime."

I looked at the Cruze. "We're not ready. Even in Connecticut this car wouldn't be ready, let alone in the Rocky Mountains."

"Where do people go around here to get that stuff fixed?"

"I think there's a little auto repair place near the gas station. Don't know if it's still open. Let's find out."

The sign said MURDOCK'S GARAGE AND TOWING. It was open, but there was only one service bay. A white pickup was up on the rack.

We got out of the Cruze, passed a red tow truck, and headed for the door. A handmade sign about winter hours was taped in the window.

Time crawled as we stood in the office, waiting to be noticed. Finally a short fellow came in, rolling a tire nearly half his height. His long, black beard made him look like an Orthodox rabbi.

"Whatcha got?" he asked.

"Chevy Cruze," I said. "Wondering if we can get it winterized."

He shook his head. "Not really. Might make it in Denver, but you're talking maybe ten feet of snow here every year. You don't even have all-wheel drive."

I resisted the urge to kick his tire. "I realize I could have made a better choice of vehicle to rent. Is there anything you *can* do?"

He shrugged. "Well, I've got that Dodge Ram on the lift. But this patch won't take long. I can get to yours in about fifteen minutes."

I gave him the key, and we sat on two of his three chairs. An issue of *Rock & Gem* magazine and an old *Motherlode Monthly* being the only reading material, we went to our phones and discovered they were surprisingly operational.

Half an hour and several forgettable websites later, the mechanic returned.

"You're done," he said. "Looked it over, checked the brakes, tested the battery, topped off the antifreeze and windshield washer fluid. No surprises. Less than a year old, after all."

"What about the tires?"

"They're not worn, but all-season radials won't be worth much with a couple feet of snow on the ground. I were you I'd put a sack of cat litter in the trunk, along with something heavy to give yourself a little traction." He handed me the keys.

"How much do I owe you?" I asked.

"No charge," he said.

"Really? But you don't have to—"

He held up a hand. "Hey, I figure you'll need that money when you bust a guardrail and go over the side in the next blizzard."

My feelings were understandably mixed.

We were about to leave when an aging green Jeep pulled up outside.

The mechanic groaned. "Oh, not this guy."

A rangy frame unfolded itself from the vehicle. It was Arthur Keebler.

"Probably wants me to buy another ad," the mechanic muttered.

"Do you have a back door?" I asked.

"Yeah, but I can't leave the shop."

"Not for you. For me."

But it was too late. Keebler power-walked through the door.

His smile perished as soon as he saw me. "Ms. Neville."

"I feel the same way," I said, and nodded toward Stephen. "This is my colleague, Stephen Ames."

"I know. Word gets around."

The mechanic stuck his hands in the pockets of his coveralls. "What can I do for you, Art?"

Keebler turned on the charm—or tried to. "Pat, I've got an opportunity for you."

"Again?"

"Almost winter. You're the only towing company in town, the only repair shop. People need to know that."

"They already do."

"Can't rest on your laurels. Look what happened to Sears and K-Mart."

"Sorry, Art. I can't afford another ad."

"Well, here's what I'm thinking. Won't cost you a penny in cash. We do a trade-out. I give you half a page, full color, you give me six months of repairs—no parts, just labor."

The mechanic shook his head. "Your Jeep looks like it's about to bite the big one."

"Three months, then."

"No can do."

Keebler rubbed his right temple with three fingers. "Have you heard the latest, Pat? *Le Coeur D'Or* may not reopen in the spring. And the Historical Museum's running out of cash. We're shutting down earlier than usual this year."

The mechanic cleared his throat. "Well, I guess we

shouldn't be airing our dirty laundry in front of visitors." He nodded toward us. "We want 'em to come back, don't we?"

Keebler snorted. "Not these particular visitors. They seem determined to drive business away."

"Huh?"

"They're writing a book that's going to make Motherlode look bad."

The mechanic eyed us, confused. "Now exactly what—"

"Oh, look at the time," I said, glancing at my watch.

His expression hovered between puzzlement and suspicion. "What's this about?"

"A difference of opinion," I said. "I'm sure Mr. Keebler will tell you all about his." Nodding for emphasis, I went for the door with Stephen following. "Thanks for looking at the car," I said.

We slipped out.

I didn't look back, being allergic to mobs of townspeople, torches, and pitchforks.

* * *

When we got in the Cruze, Stephen turned my way. "At least the guy didn't charge us."

"I think he was about to change his mind." I started the engine, having the sudden urge to be somewhere else.

"Keebler's certainly a treasure. Is he always like that?"

Steering onto the road, I shook my head. "Not quite. He seemed unusually . . . frustrated."

"So what do we do now?"

"Get a bag of cat litter, I guess."

"No, I mean about all the hostility. If enough people feel that way . . ."

"Well, the dispatcher thinks we need a gun."

"No, but maybe we should keep that hockey stick in the car."

I waved dismissively. "Mr. Keebler is a major source of greenhouse gases, but that's about it. Don't look for him to organize a lynch party."

We went silent. I watched the clouds, looking for signs of snow. I had no clue what to look for, of course. But I had to try, given my aversion to driving in anything other than perfect weather.

When we got to the Lodgepole Inn, I had an idea. "I know what to do with that rock table," I said.

"What?"

"We should put it in the trunk to give the car some weight. Not to mention the fact that I can't stand to look at it anymore."

"It's not that bad."

I peered at the sky again. "I hope we can wrap things up and leave town before the weather gets serious."

"And if we can't?"

"Then all hell breaks loose. I've read about the Donner Party. I know how these things turn out."

CHAPTER 25

About an hour later we went to lunch at the Ore Cart, our choices of restaurants dwindling as businesses shut down. I scanned the room for anyone who might be incensed by our presence. There were only an elderly couple reading *The Copper Ridge Gazette* and three men in blue-and-orange Denver Broncos jackets, none of them pointing at us or muttering imprecations.

Stephen started working on his fish sandwich. "Keebler said something about the Historical Museum."

"Closing early. Sounded like cash flow problems."

"Could we go this afternoon? I've never been."

I tried not to groan out loud. "Keebler volunteers there."

"I know. But we ought to see it before it closes."

"Marvin said it doesn't mention the murder."

"I want to see it for what it *does* mention. It's a public place, and we've got every right to be there."

I pushed a stray kernel of corn around on my plate with my fork. "It's probably not very interesting."

"You sound like me," he said. "When I was eight years old. Let's go."

I gave up. "Have it your way."

I could only hope Keebler wouldn't be at the counter.

* * *

He wasn't.

A gray-haired lady sat there, the Cranky Old Woman's more affable twin, her sweater bright purple and her eyes missing that unmistakable hint of madness. She jumped a little when we entered, apparently startled to see anyone come in.

Poking a $5 bill into the donation box, I earned a smile and a nod. We wandered inside.

No other visitors were there. The exhibits looked crowded together, as if they'd been moved from a larger building and forced to fit. Most signs were headlined in an Old Western font. All photos were black-and-white—even the most recent, dating to the days when the Victory Mine was still operational.

Here was happy prospector Edgar Auchincloss standing next to his donkey, the less happy Mary Todd. Next came a view from the cliffs in 1891, showing the sprawl of Motherlode's muddy streets, saloons, gambling parlors, and houses of ill repute.

The town's first mayor, Amos Smithouser, got a tintype portrait and a paragraph, but the more colorful Colonel Albert "Cannonball" Dunigan filled a whole four-by-eight-foot panel. Crusading newspaperman Harold P. Trayne made an appearance under the heading "A Voice Crying in the Wilderness," along with his actual crutch.

Next came a less familiar personality, a faith healer named Florence Bethany Birdwell. Pictured in front of her tent, she was described as having done a brisk business in opium during her semiannual visits, which were eventually discontinued. She fled to New York, where she continued her lurid behavior by becoming an actress. Apparently her scandal, unlike the MacIlhenny murder, was too old and entertaining to endanger the business community.

All the Gants were there somewhere, from the stiffly unsmiling Joshua to the noble Franklin to the grinning Troy, the latter pictured in sweater vest and hardhat circa 1998.

There were glass cases of rocks and minerals, the most valuable being a marble-sized gold nugget dubbed "Edgar's Egg." It rested in a plexiglass case of its own, which was bolted down and probably wired to an alarm.

Next came ore carts and pickaxes, and photos of miners wearing helmets with carbide lamps. Lined up awkwardly in a shaft, the men were no doubt developing lung disease the moment the flash powder went off.

I walked past a sign saying HEY KIDS! An arrow pointed outside to a wooden gold-panning sluice for children, but it was clogged with dead leaves. A hand-lettered card added to the sign said CLOSED.

The only interior display that tried to be interactive was a plaster model of the volcano that had formed the cliffs. A red Christmas tree bulb in the center was meant to light up when the button was pushed, but it didn't work.

Stephen leaned toward me. "Isn't this *great?*"

"Oh, yeah. I was so wrong to think otherwise."

"I know you don't mean it. That's fine. That's just your way."

We continued to meander our way through the town's past, Stephen examining every relic and reading every label while I pretended to. We were about to go when I noticed a rack of books on regional history, mostly self-published.

Three were written by Arthur Keebler, the same ones I'd

seen in Rose's shop. No doubt he displayed them in the hope of making a little money on the side.

I picked up the one about Motherlode, *The Town that Was a Treasure*.

Flipping through, I saw an autograph and handwritten message crammed between the title and signature: *May you hit the motherlode! All the best.*

I grunted. Maybe Keebler thought his inscription would make the booklet more valuable, but it looked like vandalism to me.

Wondering what the author had to say about himself, I turned the book over. According to the bio, he was a "celebrated scholar" who held "a degree in the History of the American West." The bio didn't say where he'd earned this exotic honor.

At last it was time to leave—or to be more accurate, well past time.

On the porch Stephen stretched and gazed at the horizon as if he finally understood this town. "Glad I didn't miss my chance to see it. Not the Smithsonian, but pretty cool. What did you think?"

"Enlightening."

"Oh, yeah? And what did you learn?"

"That Arthur Keebler, like so many authors I've known, has delusions of significance. And you?"

He smiled. "To never visit a museum with you again."

* * *

Back at the Lodgepole Inn, we went to our cabins. I sat on the bed and checked for phone messages. Finding none, I wondered how Marvin was doing.

Bam bam bam bam bam.

For a moment I couldn't tell where the banging was

coming from, then recognized it as an urgent knock. On a door. Mine.

I hustled to open it.

There was Stephen, looking pale. "You need to come to my cabin right away," he said.

He turned, then started to walk quickly. I yanked the door shut behind me and followed.

For a while the only sound was crunching gravel.

"What's going on?" I asked.

"I . . . you'll see."

He unlocked his door. I stepped inside after him.

I gasped. "It's a mess."

It reminded me of my own cabin a few days before. Dresser drawers pulled open. Suitcase contents strewn from bed to bathroom.

"My laptop's gone," he said.

I turned around and looked at the door locks. Again, no forced entry I could see.

"The pillows," he said. "Did you see the pillows?"

I went to the bed. They'd been ripped open, presumably with a knife. Feathers spilled everywhere.

"Maybe he was looking for something," I said.

"He didn't cut *yours* open."

"Then I don't know why. I'm not sure it really matters at this point what—"

"I think it's a message."

"What's he saying?"

"That this is not just about scaring us off anymore."

I waited for the rest.

"It's the beginning of something else. Something that doesn't stop until we're dead."

I looked around at the disarray. I couldn't think of anything encouraging to say.

Getting out my phone, I dialed the sheriff's office.

I heard Stephen close the bathroom door behind me. The fan started to hum.

If he was throwing up, I didn't want to think about it.

CHAPTER 26

A FEW MINUTES LATER STEPHEN EMERGED FROM THE bathroom. He was pale, but looked determined.

"We can't stay here anymore," he said. "At least *I* can't."

"No. Fortunately, there should be room somewhere else, now that the tourists are leaving. But first we have to get somebody from the sheriff's office here."

We grabbed our phones at the same time. "I'll work on getting another place to stay," he said as I rang Tanaka's number.

Ten minutes later, Deputy Ponytail stood in the middle of the cabin.

"This sucks, huh?" he asked, surveying the damage.

Stephen showed him the pillows and laid out his theory.

The deputy shrugged. "Maybe. Heck of a way to send a message. Guess we'd better tell Edna what happened."

We went with him to the front desk. I left the explanations to him, seeing as how he was paid to take abuse.

When she heard about the ruined pillows, the Cranky Old Woman swore under her breath. "Shoulda got the cheap foam ones," she muttered. "Feathered kind set me back a good twenty bucks apiece."

I look at the board where the keys were kept. Sure enough, the spare for Cabin Eight was gone.

I turned to the deputy. "What if you dusted the board for prints?"

He shook his head just enough to animate his ponytail. "If we had the key itself, it might make sense to dust *it*. But I doubt the board's got anything we can use."

I sighed. "You're starting to sound like Deputy Yaeger. I thought you weren't so hard-nosed."

He grinned. "Do I give that impression? Shocking." He paused. "Okay, we can dust for this print ourselves. The surface is just varnished plywood, not a fifty-year-old piece of paper."

He turned to the crone behind the desk. "Edna, I'm going to have to bring the board to the sheriff's office."

She swore again, this time with a fervor I hadn't witnessed since my cousin Ronald stepped on a nest of yellow jackets at a family reunion. "You'll have to pry it from my cold, dead hands. I know my rights. You gotta get a warrant."

He shook his head. "It's evidence."

Scowling, she found a cardboard box under the desk, dumped the keys into it, and shoved the box back under the desk. Her concern for security was admirable.

The deputy carried the board away to his squad car.

Stephen took out his phone. "Edna, I'm finding another place to stay," he said.

The old woman glared. "Good. I never want to see either of you again."

"That can be arranged," I said.

* * *

It was almost dinnertime when we checked into our new lodgings.

The Cliffview House was on the other side of town, a small place, eight rooms. Old snowshoes were mounted on the doors. It was run by a soft-spoken, middle-aged couple who didn't scowl, swear, or threaten as they checked us in. Their matching baby blue cardigans looked softer than blow-dried alpacas.

"After the last place, this is heaven," Stephen said as I handed the husband my Visa. "Not that I believe in heaven."

I skipped the chance to mention I still did. When the wife gave us our key cards, it felt like we'd reentered the 21st century.

The units were about 80 percent beige inside, with furniture and decor that must have come from some motel factory assembly line. When I brought my hockey stick in from the car, it was the only colorful item in the room.

Stephen knocked on my door at 6:00 and invited himself in. "I think I found a place for dinner," he said. "Close by. Pizza."

I brightened. It seemed like months since I'd had pizza. This new arrangement might be more than safe. It might be almost bearable.

* * *

The pizza place was only three blocks from the motel. Earth's Crust was a hole-in-the-wall eatery with the usual neon in the window, built like a brick oven and spotless inside. There was a sign on the wall:

YEAR-ROUND DELIVERY
WINTER RATE 50¢ a mile, $20 minimum

"Yikes," Stephen said.

I shrugged. "Supply and demand."

We parked ourselves in a booth with red plastic seats, filling 25 percent of the available dining area.

It seemed to be a one-man operation, unless someone else was hiding in the kitchen. The one man appeared to be in his late fifties, gray-haired and tan and strong-jawed, wearing a white apron. Bustling and breathing hard, he set one-page menus before us and tried to smile.

"Need time to decide?" he asked.

"Think so," I said.

After taking our drink orders, he hurried away.

Stephen lowered his voice. "Looks a little like Cary Grant, don't you think?"

I cocked an eyebrow. "You know about Cary Grant?"

"Hey, I'm young, not clueless."

I sipped my water. "What he looks like to *me* is a former executive who followed his dream of moving to the mountains and starting his own business. But now he's having second thoughts. He also reminds me of another upper-management type."

"Hunter? I can't imagine him doing this. It requires actual labor." He turned over his menu. "I wonder what he's doing."

"Probably planning my termination. If this book doesn't sell, he's going to have the time of his life firing me."

"Look on the bright side," he said.

"Which is?"

He set down his menu. "We may be one more break-in from getting stabbed in the dark. If that happens, you won't have to worry about your job or your money."

Just then the proprietor returned. "What can I get you?"

"A gun," I said.

His mouth dropped open.

"Just kidding," I added.

The pizza was fine, though for the rest of the evening Cary Grant kept looking at me as though I might do something rash and unprovoked. Stephen said it was my own fault.

We were about to leave when my phone came to life. It was Deputy Ponytail.

"Ms. Neville? Found something on that board from the motel."

"Really?"

"Couldn't get anything usable from the spot where your key was kept. But there was a partial print under the nail where the Cabin Eight key used to hang. A little smeared, but pretty good. I'm thinking it showed up better because it was fresh."

That was all he had, but it was enough. After thanking him, I hung up.

"Good news," I told Stephen. "We have a print from the board. Now we can compare it with the others."

"Skye's, from the book. And Gant's. And—"

"Rose's," I said, sparing him the trouble.

"I know how you feel about that. Any fool could see she'd never steal keys, break into motel rooms, or shred pillows with a knife."

I sighed. "But she might have motive. And opportunity."

A few minutes later I paid the bill. We walked into the night.

No snow yet, but the cold was intense. Each breath was visible, and probably smelled of garlic.

I tried to imagine asking Rose to roll her fingers on an inkpad.

But I couldn't.

CHAPTER 27

NEXT MORNING THERE WAS A TRACE OF SNOW ON THE ground. The sky was thick with clouds, and wind kicked up from the north.

Not caring to breakfast on pizza, we ventured to the front desk. The feminine half of Mr. and Mrs. Nice presided, smiling serenely next to a little rack that said GOURMET GORP. Overpriced packages of trail mix hung there, each bearing a green MADE IN COLORADO sticker. When we purchased four, she seemed grateful beyond words.

Back in my cabin we brewed two cups of coffee, sat in the chairs, and watched winter advance like Saddam Hussein's army on Kuwait.

"It doesn't get any better than this," Stephen said, clearly not meaning it.

I tapped some gorp into my hand. "The only thing that could improve it would be relocating to a better climate."

Munching, I found the trail mix impressive except for the sunflower seeds, which were too nutritious and obviously intended for birds. I kept chewing until I was fortified enough to bring up the subject that had kept me awake between 2:00 and 3:00 a.m.

"I've been wondering how to ask Rose for her fingerprints," I said. "And no, I won't buy another rock table to curry her favor."

He sipped his coffee, thinking. "You could say the sheriff wants them."

I shook my head. "He doesn't. She hasn't been charged with anything, much less arrested."

He folded his arms across his chest. "There's always the line about how it'll prove her innocence. When the prints don't match, she'll be in the clear."

"I was hoping for something more original."

"You don't get points for originality. You do for results."

I looked at the floor. If there was an alternative, it had eluded me.

I threw another handful of gorp into my mouth, wanting to forget.

* * *

At Simply Rose, the customers were gone.

Nearly every shelf of merchandise had a spreadsheet taped to it, making the place look like a warehouse. Rose and Dax were staring at each group of items, then tapping the tablets they held.

Turning, Rose looked reasonably glad to see us. "Are you here to help? You're just in time for inventory. Three days, then we close for the winter."

"We're editors," I said. "Numbers aren't our friends."

"Have you come to visit those fingerprints?"

"Not exactly," I said, and swallowed. "We're here . . . to get yours."

She put her tablet on the counter. "Pardon me?"

I tried to explain, using the clear-your-name defense. When I was done, Rose shrugged. "I have no problem with that."

It was my turn for eyebrow-raising. "You don't?"

"But do you have to do it *now?* If the sheriff thinks I'm guilty, won't he get my fingerprints anyway?"

"I suppose so." And I *was* tired of playing evidence technician, fiddling with used FedEx envelopes and Scotch tape and rubber gloves from Wal-Mart.

"No need to rush, I guess," I said.

She was all smiles. "Then it's settled." She paused, looking around the shop. "You know, Carolyn, I came across something during inventory that reminded me of you. Now, where was it?"

Walking to another aisle, she proceeded to bend down and lift something from a shelf. On the return trip she hid it behind her back, an impish grin on her face.

"What do you think?" she asked, bringing the item out and holding it up.

It was a fist-sized clay figurine, brown and round and unglazed, a grumpy female gnome with a pointed hat. She sat on a base with a tiny brass plaque that said THANK YOU FOR NOT SMILING.

Stephen smiled anyway. In fact, he hooted.

Rose handed it to me. "I don't mean she looks like you. It's all about the attitude."

I didn't know what to say.

Maybe that was a good thing.

* * *

When we left the shop, I carried the little clay woman to the car and carefully placed her on the floor of the back seat. Stephen said nothing.

I was about to get in when I realized I'd forgotten something. The papers with Gant's fingerprints were in Rose's fireproof box. If I gave them to the sheriff, he could compare them with the one the deputy had retrieved from the board of keys.

"Back in a minute," I said.

Rose smiled when she saw me again. I told her what I needed, and she fetched the FedEx envelope. "I hope *these* match," she said.

"So do I."

Stephen and I headed for the sheriff's office.

No deputies were at their desks. The dispatcher gave us a sorrowful nod, as if we were living on borrowed time.

The door to Tanaka's personal domain was open. He sat at his desk, reaching for the phone. Seeing us, he laughed, put down the receiver, and sauntered out.

"I was just about to call you," he said. "Knew you'd want to know right away."

I stowed the FedEx envelope under my arm and waited.

"The CBI has successfully retrieved Skye's prints from the old book." With one hand he held up some printouts; with the other, *The Prophet* in the Ziplock bag.

I couldn't help smiling. I held up my envelope. "Let's see whether these match. The suspense is killing me."

He set one of his pages, a close-up of whorls and loops, on Deputy Ponytail's desk. Next to it I placed the letter Gant had received from the lawyer.

The sheriff shook his head. "Not a match. Not even close."

I stamped my foot. "I worked *hard* to get those. I was hoping that jerk would end up in prison for *something*."

"Well, now, hold on," the sheriff said. "We've got one more possibility." He picked up another sheet. "Here's the print Deputy Ironhorse got from the board of keys at your motel."

He positioned it next to Skye's. I held my breath.

"Smeared a little," he said. "But . . . looks like a match to me."

I squinted. The image from the board was faint, but the two were practically alike.

"Oh, my God," Stephen said over my shoulder.

For a few seconds I felt dizzy.

"So Skye's alive," the sheriff said.

"And he was the one who broke into our cabins," Stephen added.

I stared at the two smudges, which were beginning to look like some kind of abstract art. "The question is, where is Skye now?"

The sheriff nodded. "And, more importantly, *who* is he?"

CHAPTER 28

Lunchtime found us back at Earth's Crust.

It wasn't that we wanted pizza again. I guess I felt sorry for the owner. Stephen said I just liked staring at a guy who looked like a movie idol and didn't have a wedding ring. I ignored him.

This time we weren't the only patrons. The owner looked slightly less depressed, due either to the increased foot traffic or because the threatening weather promised he could start delivering his product for a king's ransom.

We'd just ordered when the *1812 Overture* commenced in my tweedy brown pocket. Marvin was on the line.

"Cranberry, you've gotta help me." He was keeping his voice low.

"What's the matter?"

"I can't stand it anymore. I need to get back on the horse, you know? Got to work on the book again." He shrank his voice nearly to a whisper. "Feel like a hostage in my own house."

"What am I supposed to do?"

"Convince Tracy to let me go to Colorado."

I shut my eyes. "I can't do that. The relationship between husband and wife is sacred. It would violate God's natural order if I interfered."

"Don't give me that. You're just afraid of her."

I opened my eyes again and looked out the window. "Winter's coming. It's going to be nasty. They get about ten feet of snow a year. Cold enough to stop your heart."

There was silence. "Lot of ice, huh?"

"You hate the cold. Which is why you moved to Florida."

"Maybe I was a little hasty. Forget I said anything." He turned his volume back up. "But I want to know what's happening."

I told him about the fingerprints.

"You mean Skye's alive?"

"Looks that way."

"But if Skye killed Iris, that blows the heck out of my theory. The one in the book. I'll look like a fool."

"No, not at all. It—"

"Maybe this revised edition isn't such a great idea after all."

"Marvin, it'll help sales. People love it when an old idea gets knocked out by a new one, even if it's not an improvement."

"So what are you going to do now?"

I looked out the window again. No flakes yet. "Not sure."

"Here's what you *should* do. Have the sheriff send Skye's fingerprint to the FBI to see whether it matches one in their database. Maybe the guy was arrested for something once, somewhere. After all, he *was* a druggie."

"I'll see what I can do."

"Hang in there, girl. Let me know if—"

"Oh, wait," I said, remembering. "We could really use a fingerprint from the person who attacked you."

He gave a short laugh. "You don't say. Police said the same thing. They were pretty thorough when they went over my office. Came up dry."

"But maybe *you* wouldn't."

"I'd give it a five percent chance."

"Good. You have something else to do?"

He paused. "I guess not, now that you won't talk my lovely bride into letting me join you two."

"Then happy hunting," I said, and hung up.

* * *

Taking Marvin's advice, I called the sheriff's office.

"You again?" Tanaka asked, sounding distracted.

"That print of Skye's. Can you send it to the FBI to run through its database?"

He cleared his throat. "You know, Ms. Neville, I may not have very exciting business to attend to, but I do have a few things to do." His tone wasn't gruff, but the usual warmth was absent.

"The FBI is a little busy, too," he continued. "Despite what you may have seen on TV."

I paused, embarrassed that I'd strained his patience. "May I . . . suggest something? If you'll grant this one request, I promise not to bother you or any member of your staff for the rest of the day."

He sighed. "I'll settle for that. But I have to admit this case doesn't fascinate me quite as much as it did in the beginning. Especially when certain constituents are complaining about my 'collusion with those New Yorkers.'"

"Oh," I said, turning toward Stephen. He was watching, frowning.

"Would those constituents include Troy Gant?" I asked. "Arthur Keebler?"

"I'm not at liberty to say." He paused. "We'll get to those fingerprints soon as we can. Don't expect the FBI to respond too quickly, though."

The line went dead.

Stephen looked at me, waiting.

"We seem to be losing friends and failing to influence people," I said.

* * *

Stephen ate salad as I reran my last two conversations. My lasagna was at room temperature by the time I finished.

"The whole town's unfriending us," he said.

"Not everybody. There's still Rose. And that nice couple running our motel."

We finished our meal without much focus or cleverness, talking mostly about the weather. When we were done, we put on our coats and steeled ourselves to face it.

Stephen grunted as soon as the door opened. The wind was picking up, and flakes were starting to fall.

"It's the driving I hate most about winter," I said, climbing into the car. "Even at home."

He snapped the latch on his seatbelt. "At least you stay in practice. I've gotten so used to using the train I've practically forgotten how to turn the key."

Flicking on the wipers, I eased out of the parking lot. "The worst part is trying to drive on ice."

"Maybe having the rock table in the back will help."

Suddenly I remembered the mechanic's advice. "Forgot to get cat litter," I said.

"The market must have it."

Approaching the next intersection, I clicked my blinker to turn left. A space cleared just as the light turned yellow, and I took the opportunity. "I guess we should get the biggest size they—"

"Look out!" Stephen yelled.

Out of nowhere something large and white bore down on us. A massive horn blared over a *screeeeeech*. My heart stumbled.

With no room to spare we made the turn, the other vehicle barreling down the street. I pulled over in front of a vacant storefront, my ears ringing.

"Did you see it?" I asked.

"Didn't you?" His voice cracked. "A white pickup. Gone now."

I swallowed. "It's always a pickup. Think they own the—"

"Wait a minute. A big vehicle, right?"

For a moment I didn't know what he meant.

"Isn't that what the stoner kid said? Whoever broke into our cabins drove something big?"

I shook my head. "The driver couldn't have planned it that way. Didn't know we'd be there, or that we'd be turning left. Besides, you don't cause a head-on collision to get rid of someone. Too much risk, even if you're bigger."

He sank back into the seat. "Then you think it was just lousy driving."

"Yes."

"Yours or his?"

"*Mine?* How could it be *mine?*"

"Well, you *were* taking a chance on that light."

I opened my mouth to reply, but my head was starting to throb. Too much adrenaline with nowhere to go.

"Cat litter," I muttered. "We were on our way to get some."

I pulled back into traffic, not that there was much. I tried to glance in every possible direction, feeling exposed, vulnerable.

This was not a good sign. Our escape had been too narrow.

And the ice was yet to come.

CHAPTER 29

THERE WERE ONLY TWO 20-POUND PLASTIC JUGS OF CAT LITTER left. I wrestled one from the shelf, resisting the urge to buy both. I didn't want someone else's excretory disaster on my conscience.

Stephen picked out a quart of allegedly homemade minestrone in the tiny deli section, then stocked up on granola bars. "Cheaper than gorp," he said.

Still shaky from the near-miss, I drove to the gas station to make sure the tank was full.

"Oh, crap," Stephen said. "Look at the line."

There must have been a dozen vehicles, a hefty percentage of the local driving population. I squeezed the Cruze behind a Toyota 4Runner. "Probably worried the station will run out. Which it will, thanks to our lemming behavior."

"And all those gas cans," he said. About half the drivers were filling red plastic containers at the pumps, probably for snowblowers.

Turning off the ignition, I settled back. Despite all the

movement in front of us, it was quiet. Snow was starting to accumulate on the windshield.

Something caught my eye two cars ahead. An old, green Jeep. I groaned.

"Keebler," I said.

"Well, he needs gas, too."

I shut my eyes. "I just hope I won't end up at a pump near him and have to carry on a civil conversation."

For the next five minutes cars and trucks jockeyed for position, shifting like squares in one of those hellish sliding tile puzzles. I tried to predict when and where we'd end up, but the effort just summoned my previous headache.

Ultimately, of course, we landed next to Keebler and his jeep.

He didn't notice me at first. With a sour expression he filled a gallon gas can, the old-fashioned metal kind. When he started on his tank, he saw me.

I looked away, trying not to catch his eye or breathe the fumes.

An edgy silence followed as the numbers on the pump added up. Finally I holstered the nozzle and tore off the receipt.

"Consider the bright side," I heard Keebler say behind me.

I turned around. "Excuse me?"

"There'll be plenty of fuel for everybody when the tourists stop coming. Of course, when that happens the station itself will have to shut down."

I stuffed the receipt in my pocket. "Maybe you should share that observation with the sheriff. I understand you've become one of his economic advisors."

He tore off his own receipt. "I wouldn't know anything about that."

After climbing into the Jeep, he pulled away. Within seconds another vehicle had taken his place.

That was fine with me. If I never saw Keebler again, it would be too soon.

* * *

Snow was falling in earnest as we drove back to the Cliffview House. The wipers could barely keep up. Despite the posted speed of 40, I kept ours at 25. A flatbed truck tailgated me, its headlights glaring in irritation.

"Just remember," Stephen said, his voice tight. "If you start to slide, turn in the direction you're sliding. I've never done it, but that's what they say."

"There's no ice yet," I said, trying to sound casual.

He adjusted the heating vent on his side, which probably didn't help. "I wonder how long we can survive on a little soup and some granola bars. Maybe I should have bought more."

"We can always have pizza delivered. If I can afford it, which I can't."

After what seemed like half an hour but undoubtedly wasn't, we pulled into the motel lot. There were about three inches on the ground. Blinking away the snowflakes, we headed for our respective rooms and hunkered down.

* * *

Darkness fell at 6:54 p.m.

We sat in my room, having just finished our minestrone and granola bars. Now we watched the snow pile up.

I sipped coffee, hoping it wouldn't keep me awake tonight. That was the storm's job, after all.

"Looks like nearly six inches already," Stephen said.

"Maybe we shouldn't look. It only increases the stress

level." I got up and pulled the curtains closed. Our world was now warm, beige, placid, safe.

He finished his coffee, then looked in vain for another packet.

"Do you still think the truck was trying to hit us?" I asked.

He shrugged. "Guess not. But somebody wants to send us home."

"Isn't Gant." I thought for a moment. "Too bad we don't have a better photo of Skye. We could age it like they do the kids on milk cartons, see what he might look like now."

"Or she."

I raised an eyebrow.

"Skye might be transgender now. Could have changed his name to . . . Well, *Skyler* is a woman's name, isn't it?"

I shook my head. "I've heard some pretty unlikely scenarios, but this takes the—"

All at once the lights went out.

Every one, right down to the red dot below the TV screen. With the curtains closed, the black was infinite.

Seconds later a faint, white rectangle appeared in Stephen's vicinity, seeming to float in midair. It took me a moment to recognize his cell phone.

He swore. "Wish I had a flashlight," he added.

"Must be the storm." Finding my own phone, I followed suit. There was just enough illumination to get me to the window, where I lifted the curtain.

Streetlights, of which there were no more than four, seemed unaffected. I could barely make them out through the blowing snow. "Strange," I said.

"What?"

"Looks like the motel's the only place without power."

A chill swept my chest, the kind that had nothing to do with temperature.

"What's going on?" he asked.

I didn't answer.

But something was very wrong.

CHAPTER 30

PICKING MY WAY BACK TO THE CHAIR, I BASHED MY knee. "*Ow.*"

"What happened?"

With a grunt I lowered myself to the sitting position. "Oh, I just—"

There was a thump somewhere, and a click.

WHOOM!

The whole place seemed to explode, the door flinging inward, nearly off its hinges, blasting the room with a flood of arctic wind and a miasma of flakes.

Gasping, I reared back.

Light, too much of it, flared from the doorway, blinding. A flashlight, the brightest I'd ever seen.

The door slammed shut. For a long time the only thing I could hear was breathing—mine, Stephen's. And someone else's.

I squinted. The flashlight was unwavering. So was the intruder's silence.

Finally I found my voice, or part of it. "Who is it?"

The stranger said nothing.

I swallowed, then sat up. "I know who you are," I said.

It was only half a bluff. The pieces were starting to come together. I decided to take a chance.

"Want to know how I know?"

Silence.

"When Marvin came back to look into the MacIlhenny murder again, he told three people he was here. The sheriff, George Svoboda, and you."

Still no reply.

"It wasn't the sheriff, of course. And George wasn't up to killing anybody. But you were." I paused. "You have a large vehicle. The kind the housekeeper at the Lodgepole Inn saw the day you stole the key to my cabin."

The wind whistled outside. There was a creaking sound as the intruder stepped closer.

"We've seen the fingerprints of practically everyone else in this town, but not yours. Not your current prints, anyway. But I saw the message you wrote over your autograph in your pamphlets at the museum. Not quite like the notes in Skye's old copy of *The Prophet*. But now that I think about it, close enough."

Silence again.

"Your booklet was informative, Mr. Keebler. But it left me wondering. Where does a person get a degree in the History of the American West? And why didn't your author bio say anything about where you lived or what you did before moving here?"

The flashlight wobbled. Finally I heard a throat being cleared.

"Since you know so much," Keebler said flatly, "you tell me."

"I just don't understand what happened to Skye."

He gave an impatient sigh. "After I left here, I knocked around a couple of ski resorts. Fooled around at a little experimental college in California for two years. Altered my consciousness a few too many times. We were all ridiculous in those days."

"Not all of us," I said.

"But we all change, don't we? I'm not the only guy who traded his bong for a briefcase. Got into being an entrepreneur. This town was the only place I ever really fit, so I did it here. By then nobody could recognize me."

"Remember your old friend Jimmy Fields?"

"Yeah. The man's a basket case now."

"He told us you dropped acid. I'm no expert on drugs, but I'm told they can make a person do strange things."

"What can I say? You heard right. I still get headaches. Blacked out once when I was driving. Almost drove over the side of Highway 26."

I looked away from the light and closed my eyes. The intense afterimage wouldn't go away. "Headaches weren't the worst of it, were they? You did something nobody in his right mind would even consider."

He said nothing.

"Iris didn't just stop breathing. You choked her with your bare hands. Not the kind of thing a peaceful guy like Skye would do."

"What do you want from me, an anti-drug commercial? 'Okay, kids, just say no.' I was young and stupid."

There was a long pause.

"But why *Iris*?"

"I don't remember much about that night, alright? Walked back to my tent after my shift at the bar. Must have had a flashback."

"Do you know what she was doing out there so late?"

"Probably going home after seeing one of her boyfriends.

I heard rumors from two people at work that she was involved with at least one guy."

"So you strangled her."

"She was in the wrong place, wrong time. Wasn't her fault. Wasn't mine."

I shook my head.

The light winked out for a moment, then cast a circle on the carpet. There was a metallic sound, like something being tapped and unscrewed. Then a smell, sharp and overwhelming.

Gasoline.

I coughed, then remembered what had happened at the gas station.

Keebler hadn't been out to refill a snowblower after all.

* * *

He seemed to be holding the flashlight with one hand and unscrewing the gas can's cap with the other. The odor got stronger.

"It's too bad the whole place has to go," he said. "But that's not my fault, either. The volunteer fire department isn't known for its response time."

The circle of light jumped around as he lifted a coil of rope from his shoulder. "Now, if you'll take this. . ."

Just then I remembered the hockey stick. It was by the bed. Where was the bed?

Still sitting in the chair, I felt around behind me. *No, that's the lamp.* Then to my left. *There.* Nothing else felt quite like adhesive tape wrapping a handle.

Grabbing it, I swung wide. But all I hit was air.

I tried again, this time knocking the flashlight from Keebler's grasp. The circle of light shrank to a cone on the floor.

Keebler stumbled backward. "Son of a—"

Reaching down, he fumbled for the flashlight. But Stephen snatched it off the floor and shone it in his eyes.

With both hands I took hold of the hockey stick and shoved it into the center of his puffy, gray parka. He grunted, falling backward. The gas can tipped over. The vapor was choking.

I gave him one more whack with the stick, then scrambled for the door. Stephen was right behind me, still holding the flashlight. He pointed it over my shoulder at the doorknob.

We tumbled out, straight into the subzero wind. The shock cut off my breath. Neither of us had a coat on, but there was no time to do anything about it.

The air was thick with a rush of flakes. Despite the flashlight's impressive caliber, I couldn't see a thing.

Reaching into my pocket, I felt the fob for the Cruze and thumbed the unlock button twice. Two faint flashes of red hinted where I should go.

I headed in that direction, the legs of my pants already sodden to mid-shin. Slush was filling my shoes.

I was almost on top of the car when I saw it. Flinging the door open, I threw the hockey stick in the back and climbed in. Stephen clambered into the passenger side, still clinging to the flashlight.

I turned the key and the vehicle sprang to life.

"Hang on!" I said, not even knowing what that meant under the circumstances.

I'd find out soon enough.

* * *

The shivering began in earnest.

Maybe I'd been trembling the whole time, but now that

we were seat-belted and immobilized, the quaking went into high gear. I reached for the heater's controls, but knew the engine needed time to warm up. The last thing we needed was to import even more of the great outdoors.

I looked in the rearview mirror. All I could see were two headlights. They weren't moving yet.

Oh, *now* they were.

Toward us.

The snow was getting deeper, nearly eight inches by my reckoning. Already our wheels were starting to spin, then catch, then slide sideways.

"We sh-should . . . head for the sheriff's office," I said, my teeth chattering.

Stephen snapped off the flashlight and hugged himself. He sniffed, his nose apparently running. "Which w-way is it? I can't see a thing."

I squinted to the left. "Are those streetlights?"

His whole body seemed to be shaking. "Can't tell."

Mirage or not, they offered the only clue. I steered in their direction.

My fingers were losing sensation on the wheel. I fumbled with the heater buttons, but the resulting stream of tepid air made little difference.

He twisted back around to face the front, then wiped his nose with his sleeve. "God, what I wouldn't g-give for my coat. Or yours. I can't believe this is happening."

The windshield was fogging up, so I pushed another button. Slowly it cleared, but we still couldn't see more than 10 feet ahead.

"I don't suppose you can . . . dial 911 or something," I said.

"Already tried. No reception." He twisted in his seat and looked out the back. "He's gaining on us. We can't keep this up."

I shook my head, the rest of my body quivering less voluntarily. "Of course . . . we can."

"How?"

I tapped the dashboard.

"We've got . . . plenty of gas."

Unfortunately, we had nowhere to go.

CHAPTER 31

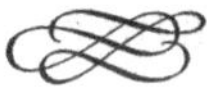

We kept going, but just barely. Soon we were inching our way.

On the positive side, the heater was starting to do its job. Maybe we could thaw out before Keebler burned us to death.

"What happened to the streetlights?" Stephen asked. "This can't be right."

According to the rearview mirror, the Jeep was practically on our bumper. I caught a glimpse of Keebler, but couldn't make out his face. I wondered whether he was thinking this was all too easy. We *were* pathetic, not giving up when the end was pretty much preordained.

The terrain started to tilt uphill. The wheels spun again, making that futile whirring sound. This time the spinning lasted longer and the catching all but disappeared.

Then, all at once, it was gone.

The Cruze was high-centered, stuck.

Swallowing, I killed the engine. I left the lights on. Eventually I'd have to turn them off but needed to know what was going on out there for as long as possible.

We said nothing for a moment, just looked out the windows.

"What now?" Stephen asked.

I wondered what Jack London might do. Whatever it was, it wouldn't involve cat litter.

I pushed the lock button on my door. All the locks clacked. "We should stay in the car. If he had a gun, he'd have used it by now."

Keebler had his lights on, too. Nearly a minute passed before he opened his door and climbed out, bundled in his parka, the flapping hood obscuring most of his face, the tops of his green rubber boots just above the snow's surface. The gas can still hung from his leather-gloved hand.

"Didn't that spill on the floor?" Stephen asked. "How much do you think he has left?"

Keebler looked around as if to make sure no one could see, which no one possibly could. Planting his steps deep, he moved closer.

As if to answer Stephen's question, he raised the container and began to splash its contents on the Cruze, starting with our gas tank.

I cringed. "Not the rental car!" I glanced at the paperwork I'd stored in the door. "I didn't get coverage for this."

Keebler kept splattering. When he got to the front doors, he stopped. Apparently the can was empty.

But to set the car on fire, that would be more than enough.

* * *

Hitting the unlock button, I proceeded to grab the hockey stick.

The instant we threw the doors open, the wind was everywhere, heaving, roaring. The cold took charge, more piercing than ever. I tried to blink away the snow that caught in my lashes.

I raised the hockey stick.

But Keebler had a surprise. He hadn't run out of fuel at all.

The first splash was aimed at my face. Just in time I squeezed my eyes shut, but couldn't keep from getting a noseful. Gagging, I pitched forward into the snow.

I managed not to vomit but spat at least five or six times. Finally I stood up, unsteady, still holding the hockey stick.

The whistling wind yanked most of the smell away. But the fuel, instantly evaporating, had made my face even colder.

Stephen was bending over, coughing.

Gripping the end of the stick, I swung again, trying to knock the can from Keebler's hand.

But my own hands were numb, slick with melted ice. Despite the adhesive tape, the stick slipped from my grasp and sailed into the night.

* * *

Keebler jammed the can into the snow. He pulled a cigarette lighter from his pocket. It was big, stainless steel, the wind-proof kind.

Shaking, Stephen stood up. He turned my way. "The table!" he yelled over the wind's howl.

"What?"

He pointed at the Cruze's trunk.

The rock table. It was so heavy, maybe . . .

I fumbled for my keys, then dropped them in the snow, then fished them out.

My fingers were like wood as I unlocked the trunk.

The lid flew up. Startled, Keebler took a step backward. He bobbled his lighter but caught it at the last second.

I seized one end of the table. Stephen took the other.

"Now!" he shouted.

Keebler flicked the lighter. Defying the storm, a flame appeared.

With a simultaneous groan we hauled the table from the trunk, up and out, wood and steel whacking each other on the way.

Keebler took another step back, dropping the lighter, but he was too late. The table caught him full in the face, stone against bone. Arms flailing, he went down backward in the snow, blood running from his nose.

Not knowing what else to do, I sat on the table, trying to hold him down. He was remarkably vigorous for a man of his age. But he'd been walking all his life, hadn't he?

Squeezing the table legs, I raised myself about a foot. Then I dropped back down like a sack of cement, punching him deeper into the snow.

I figured I'd knocked the air from him, but he kept writhing. I resisted the urge to repeat my action, not wanting to kill him unless I had to.

I sat there panting, the wind spiriting away the clouds of breath before I could see them. Stephen scrambled clumsily through the snow to the Jeep, then returned with the coils of rope Keebler had meant to use on us.

Our numbed fingers made it almost impossible to tie the knots, but we managed to truss his hands and feet. The blood from his nose made the snow look like raspberry sorbet.

The wailing wind drowned most of his expletives as we dragged him to the back seat of the Jeep. After climbing into the front seat ourselves, we cranked up the heat as high as it would go.

"The table," Stephen said. "It's still out there."

I groaned. "Do we have to keep it?"

"We can't just leave it here."

"Why not?"

"I don't know. Never mind. We'll get it later."

I nodded, hoping we'd never find this spot again.

He looked out his window. "Where are we?"

I swiveled around. "Can't get my bearings. No telling when this is going to let up, either."

He tried 911 again, but it didn't work.

I shook my head. "I hate to say it, but I almost wish we had GPS."

"Wouldn't help. No cell service."

We quieted, listening to the wind and our heartbeats. Even Keebler was silent.

I swallowed. My theology told me I was never alone, but it sure didn't feel that way.

CHAPTER 32

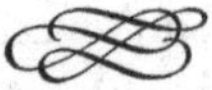

THOUGH I DIDN'T KNOW WHAT TO DO, THERE SEEMED NO alternative to doing something.

After clearing my throat a few times and trying unsuccessfully not to grind the gears, I began to back the Jeep downhill, inch by agonizing inch.

Stephen unhooked his seatbelt, turned around, and knelt in his seat, peering into the blackness. "I can barely see anything," he said.

"Good to know."

"Okay, wait. There's a tree behind you. Go to your . . . left."

I turned the wheel.

"Okay, straight back."

"This is going to take forever," I said.

After what seemed like a month, we'd covered about 50 feet.

"I think you're clear for maybe the next ten yards," he said.

I almost relaxed. I let the Jeep roll a little more freely.

"Okay, I—*no! No!*"

I hit the brake, but we slid another few feet. The rear of the Jeep seemed to drop. There was a thump.

I hit the accelerator. The wheels started to spin.

I gulped.

"You're sort of hanging over the edge," he said, his voice tense.

"The edge of *what?*"

"It's like an embankment. All dark past the edge, so I can't tell how deep it is."

The wheels were still spinning. I knew they couldn't keep it up forever.

"I knew we should have brought the table," he said. "You never did like—"

There was a groan from the back seat. "Twist the wheel as sharply as you can," Keebler said, sounded as if his nose was plugged up.

"Which way?"

"Doesn't matter. But then stop, so you don't make a U-turn and go over."

I jerked the wheel to the right. There was a crunch of snow, and the Jeep leapt forward.

"Now stop!"

I mashed the brake. We halted.

Everyone exhaled, even Keebler. "Idiot," he added.

Steering away from the abyss, I peered into the night. The snow seemed a bit lighter now. There was a hint of brightness in the distance, now that we faced another direction.

"The cliffs," Stephen said. "Go that way."

I did so. A few minutes later we passed a SPEED 35 sign, the upper half of the message hidden by snow. We were on a road.

The luminous cliffs became our Holy Grail as we maintained a steady clip of about nine miles per hour. Where the cliffs were, the Cliffview House couldn't be far away.

Soon Keebler was rustling again. "You taking me to the sheriff's office?"

"That's the plan," I said.

He sniffed. "You've got nothing to convict me. No proof."

"We will, once we have your fingerprints. I'm sure the sheriff won't neglect to get them. It won't even matter whether the FBI has them in its database, or whether Marvin can find any in his office."

"It wasn't murder, anyway," he said. "It was the acid. No premeditation. Don't think I haven't looked into *that* in the last fifty years."

"You left a young woman dead and an old man in a coma. I imagine they'll find something to charge you with."

He sniffed again. I couldn't tell whether it was out of disdain or because his nose was broken.

We maneuvered the rest of the way without further conversation, not seeing a single vehicle. By the time we passed the Cliffview House, whose lights were still off, we were going a confident 15 miles per hour. The wind had slackened, and my socks were beginning to turn from dripping to damp.

The sheriff's office was the only place open. Even the bar was closed.

Stephen looked at his watch. "That can't be right. Says it's only 10:09. Feels like two in the morning."

"Time flies when you're being threatened with immolation," I said.

Leaving Keebler in the Jeep, we braved the cold and went inside.

Deputy Crabb was the only one present, talking on the phone to a Mrs. Allenby, whose satellite dish apparently had blown off her house. He told her she needed to call the company, a suggestion she didn't seem to like.

When he finally hung up, he looked us over. "This must be pretty important."

We took turns telling him what had happened. The more we said, the closer his eyebrows got to his hairline.

"So that's why I smell gas," he said. "Keebler's in the car right now?"

I nodded. "He's all yours."

The deputy checked his sidearm and pulled on his parka. "If the phone rings, take a message. I can't order it, but I can urge you to do your civic duty."

"We do solemnly swear," Stephen said wearily.

A few minutes later the deputy was back, holding Keebler by the arm. "We'll get somebody to look at that nose eventually. In the meantime, you're under arrest."

We listened to the usual speech about remaining silent. This time it sounded sweet, like a wedding ceremony.

The deputy took out the magnetic powder and recorded the prints. Then he ushered the prisoner into the cell which, fortunately, the singing drunk no longer called home.

* * *

Exhausted, we slept late the next morning.

Rising from the bed, I groaned and flopped back onto the mattress. My back and shoulders ached, probably from hitting Keebler with the table.

I couldn't remember whether I'd thanked God for that ugly piece of furniture, let alone that we hadn't been prematurely cremated. I took care of the matter while waiting for my muscles to stop twitching.

A whiff of gasoline hung in the air. Mr. and Mrs. Nice had done their best just before midnight, but something more potent than vinegar and baking soda seemed to be in order.

The smell clung to me as well, and probably to the tweedy brown editor's blazer I'd left in a heap on the floor. Maybe it always would.

Glancing next to my bed where the hockey stick had once resided, I sighed. It had served me loyally, and I felt its loss already.

My second effort to rise proved painful but successful. Shuffling to the window, I proceeded to peek around the curtain's edge. The storm was over, the sky a bitter blue. Nearly a foot of white topped every car in the lot.

Just then a large, gray snowplow with a CITY OF MOTHERLODE logo on the side, perhaps the only such truck in existence, thundered past. Its blade cast aside a spate of snow, most notably onto Keebler's Jeep.

I was about to lower the curtain when another vehicle followed, a red truck emblazoned with MURDOCK'S GARAGE AND TOWING. A smaller blade was affixed this time, and I could see the silhouette of a prodigiously bearded driver in the cab. Pulling into the lot, he commenced clearing it.

The room phone rang behind me. It was Stephen.

"I can't get out of bed," he said, sounding pained. "At least I don't want to."

"Don't tell me. You pulled a muscle when we hit Keebler with the table."

"How did you know?"

"I've got the same problem. If I could get up, so can you. I suggest the Ore Cart for breakfast."

He grunted. "I'll be glad when I can get a *real* meal again, like a ladleful of blue cheese dressing in the Pendleton cafeteria. But I'll be at your room in half an hour."

* * *

To my surprise, the crowd at the restaurant was a literal crowd. There was a 15-minute wait.

"They must think this weather is normal," I said. "I could never live in a town like this."

When our turn came I ordered the Gold Rush Flapjacks—plus a side of bacon, this being a special occasion.

Stephen shook his head. "Bacon kills."

"Just hastening my inevitable decline."

When our food came, Stephen reached across the table, stole a slice of bacon, and took a bite. "To slow your inevitable decline," he explained.

I looked around the room. "Where are all the townspeople coming up and congratulating us on our great accomplishment?"

"Maybe word will get around. Not in Keebler's magazine, but at least the Copper Ridge Paper."

I took a fork to my pancakes. "We'll have to tell Marvin, of course. And Hunter."

"And Rose."

Wincing, I put down the fork.

What was I going to do about Rose?

CHAPTER 33

IT TOOK 24 HOURS FOR THE MECHANIC TO GET AROUND TO towing our rental car from the forest. Locating it was the biggest problem, but his search was successful. Unfortunately, he also spotted what was left of the rock table and insisted on bringing it back.

The Cruze still reeked of gasoline, especially inside, but was drivable. A long scrape marred the passenger side, probably from tree branches, and one taillight was broken. When I came to take it to the motel, the mechanic kept telling me I was lucky to be alive. For the sake of time, I didn't argue.

At the Cliffview House I called Marvin. Before I could tell him what happened, he sighed.

"I tried, Cranberry, I really did. But I couldn't find a single print in my office."

"Just as well," I said, and unraveled what I considered to be the book-worthy saga of the last 24 hours. If it wasn't, I'd never recoup the $13,000 or so I'd spent in the last two months.

When my narrative was done, he snorted. "The old guy at

the museum was Skye? And I missed it? Man, maybe it's time for me to take up stuff like tai chi and model railroading."

"First you've got a book to write. We'll get in touch next week."

"Just like old times," he said, and hung up.

Finally I dialed Hunter. He was in a meeting. I left no message, there being too much to say. I decided to wait until we got back to New York.

And now, seventy-two hours later, Stephen and I were checking out of the Cliffview House, turning in our key cards to Mr. and Mrs. Nice. They were wearing matching sweaters, brown and orange, with Thanksgiving turkeys on them.

"Sorry about the room," I said. "I'm sure the smell will be gone eventually."

"And you might be able to salvage the door," Stephen added.

The husband smiled bravely. "Insurance should cover the damage."

"We'll show our appreciation with favorable reviews on Yelp and TripAdvisor," Stephen said.

"And by never returning," I added. Mr. Nice couldn't hide his gratitude.

We loaded the back seat with our luggage, since the rock table was hogging the trunk.

I shut the door. "Are we forgetting anything? Said goodbye to the sheriff . . . got our laptops back . . ."

"What about Rose?"

"I guess . . . we have to do something."

"We can give her the table."

A few minutes later we pulled up to the little green bungalow. Rose smiled when she answered the doorbell. She was in a rubbery gray sweat suit, looking moist and slightly winded.

"I heard what happened," she said when we'd sat on the couch. "Skye was here all this time." She shook her head. "I wish my folks could see this. Not looking forward to the trial, though."

I bit my lip. "Maybe it'll bring some . . . closure?"

Rose shrugged. "I don't know." She paused. "One of the deputies found the hatbox at Mr. Keebler's place. But they can't return it because it's evidence."

A long silence followed. I looked at the floor. I didn't know how to say goodbye. Rose had some real problems. The drinking. The aloneness. The uncertain future. Maybe she just seemed too much like me.

I cleared my throat and looked up. "Thanks for the gnome. She's in my suitcase."

"You saved me having to count it as inventory."

"And that rock table saved our lives. It's in our trunk."

"What are you going to do with it?"

"We can't take it on the plane. Maybe you could resell it. It got pretty wet, though, and it might take a while to get all that blood off . . ."

She looked a little nauseated. "I'll probably give it to the thrift shop. If they open in the spring."

She stood up, and we did the same. Suddenly she put her arms around me.

"Take care, Carolyn," she said softly.

"Come visit me in New York."

I followed Stephen outside. After muscling the table from the trunk and into her garage, we climbed into what remained of the car and drove away.

* * *

The highway to Denver was mostly cleared of snow. The Cruze did well, probably because it was all downhill from Crystal County.

In Buena Vista we stopped for gas. I held my breath as I pumped it, the smell bringing back an unpleasant memory.

Climbing back into the car, I felt something in the left pocket of my slacks. I fished it out.

It was a polished stone. Shining, cloudy, with black scribbles running through it.

"What's that?" Stephen asked.

"Some kind of quartz. George Svoboda gave it to me."

"Oh."

He settled back and closed his eyes. I started the engine.

The highway stretched before us like an invitation. The azure sky was limitless.

After rubbing the stone with my thumb, I returned it to my pocket.

I wondered what things would be like a year from now.

For Marvin's book.

For Stephen.

For Rose.

For me.

* * *

One year later, more or less, I sat in my office on a Tuesday night. I still had the same laptop, which glowed on the old-fashioned blotter in front of me.

I was studying sales figures. *Darkness at Dawn,* revised and updated, had been released the month before. Initial sales were promising. The review in *Publishers Weekly* was starred, and there was talk of a movie, though it probably would never be more than talk.

Marvin was touring, doing book signings, despite the fact

that everyone knew signings didn't move merchandise unless you were The King of Horror or The Hardest Working Man in Show Business. His lovely bride, he said, was nagging him to come home so she could nag him in person.

Hunter, meanwhile, had just celebrated his sixth anniversary by handing out 230 T-shirts silkscreened with the words I'M A HUNTER FOR EXCELLENCE, most of which probably had been donated directly to Goodwill by their recipients. He'd also given up on winning his bet, conceding I wasn't going to lose my job. This time.

Stephen hadn't changed except that he was going out with a performance artist named Ariel who dealt mostly in Bolivian flute music and shipping herself in boxes from one town to another. It didn't seem serious, though.

I hadn't been seeing anybody regularly. I'd dated Jim Bannister, the tall lawyer at church, a few more times. He didn't seem to have anything major wrong with him, but in the end I couldn't pretend the "weaker sex" thing didn't exist.

Maybe I was too picky. That's what Mikki said. She'd stopped seeing the Uber driver and started spending time with a radiologist. But he was always on call.

I'd been happy to hear Troy Gant had lost the Victory Mine. *The Denver Post* reported the place might be added to the State Register of Historic Properties, thereby preserving it for future generations of tourists who had nothing better to do than ride rattling elevators and chew bubble gum pellets shaped like gold nuggets.

Arthur Lawrence Keebler had been convicted of manslaughter and attempted murder and was starting to serve a 45-year sentence. His trial ensured the reelection of Sheriff Woody Tanaka, who testified with enough crinkly-eyed charisma to have Colorado pundits speculating he could enter the next gubernatorial race.

Rose, meanwhile, had taken Keebler's place at the Historical Museum. She was adding an exhibit about the MacIlhenny case, including the hatbox.

Rumor had it she was going out with the owner of Earth's Crust Pizza.

I shut down the laptop and rubbed my eyes.

The polished stone from George Svoboda sat to the left of the blotter. I picked it up, held it to the fluorescent light overhead, and set it back down.

Three days ago I'd seen on the Motherlode city website that George himself had passed away, age 93. I planned to keep that rock, maybe forever.

According to George, after all, some people swore it brought good luck.

Though as he'd also said, those people were full of *posetilost*. Foolishness.

He was right, of course.

But maybe they were, too.

A LOOK AT: MURDER AT CLUSTER SPRINGS RACEWAY BY JOHN THEO JR.

A deadly auto accident at a southern Virginia racetrack draws private investigator Brandon Hall into a new case. When young race car driver Drew Schilling dies in a fiery crash, his politician father hires Brandon to investigate. Virginia Senator Gregory Schilling believes his son's death was not an accident, but a politically motivated murder.

With the help of friends, Brandon uncovers evidence which ties the raceway death to the rapidly changing political landscape in the United States. Radicalized groups, promoting violence on college campuses and cities, have found their way into rural southern Virginia. Enter the corrupt world of Washington DC politics, old Dixieland families, and the volatile culture wars unfolding within the United States.

Brandon Hall is an army veteran who owns a cattle farm in the quiet southern town of Nathalie, Virginia. It has been just over a year since the death of his two-year-old son at the hands of a drunk driver. Together with his wife Annie, and ten-year-old daughter Emily, the Halls struggle to recover from the devastating loss. Each day is a spiritual, emotional, and financial struggle. To supplement the farm income, Brandon moonlights as a private investigator and contract diver. Murder at Cluster Springs Raceway is a tale straight from Virginia, and national, headlines.

AVAILABLE NOW!

ABOUT THE AUTHOR

John Duckworth is a novelist, editor, playwright, scriptwriter, cartoonist, and father of twins. After earning his bachelor's degree at Linfield College, he spent 35 years in the publishing industry as a curmudgeonly editor, product developer, and author, working with people like Ken Blanchard, Dr. Kevin Leman, Richard Foster, and Calvin Miller, producers like VeggieTales, organizations like Focus on the Family and companies like Random House, Thomas Nelson, NavPress, Group Publishing, Zondervan and Rainfall Toys.

After producing nearly 250 issues of weekly publications *Power for Living* and *FreeWay*, he created seven multi-volume series of youth ministry resources. He's edited or rewritten hundreds of books, articles, and lesson plans.

www.ingramcontent.com/pod-product-compliance
Lightning Source LLC
LaVergne TN
LVHW030919080826
845145LV00013B/2959

* 9 7 8 1 6 3 9 7 7 0 9 4 6 *